UNSUITABLE BETROTHAL

LADIES, LOVE, AND MYSTERIES

JOYCE ALEC

Unsuitable Betrothal

Text Copyright © 2020 by Joyce Alec

First printing, 2020

Publisher
Love Light Faith, LLC
400 NW 7th Avenue, Unit 825
Fort Lauderdale, FL 33311

LOVE LIGHT FAITH

Receive a FREE inspirational romance eBook by visiting our website and signing up for our mailing list. Click the link or enter www.LoveLightFaith.com into your browser.

The newsletter will also provide information on upcoming books and special offers.

"Hannah?"

Miss Hannah Seymour closed her eyes, her fingers tightening on the book she had been reading. She already knew what was to come, hating that her father had come to demand answers to the very same questions he had asked her every single day thus far.

"Yes, Father?" she asked as Viscount Addington entered the library, his brows low and his eyes dark with irritation. "Is there something you wanted?"

He stood directly in front of her, his arms folded across his chest. "Hannah. You have not had any callers today, I think."

Sighing inwardly, she looked up at her father. "I have not," she said softly, knowing that her father did not refer to Lord Paxton and Miss Hawkins, who had come to call earlier that day, but rather was wanting confirmation that she had not received any *gentlemen* callers.

"And do you expect to have any?"

Hannah dropped her gaze and looked at the floor, feeling that sense of creeping shame come over her again. For a few short weeks, she had felt a sense of anticipation, believing that there was a faint spark of hope in her future, only for it to be snuffed out without warning. "I do not expect any this afternoon, Father, no," she said, a little dully. "I am to go out this evening, however."

Lord Addington snorted but did not make any particular comment. Hannah said nothing also, keeping her gaze fixed to the floor as heat climbed into her cheeks, waiting for her father to pronounce his judgment. As the Season had progressed, her father had taken every opportunity to ask her if she had any particular gentlemen callers. It was a constant reminder that she was as yet without any sort of interest from any gentlemen whatsoever and that, should this Season end as it had begun, she would find herself wed to a gentleman of her father's choosing. And, most likely, it would be someone that he needed to be in his debt in one way or another. It was all about what was best for Lord Addington, rather than for her. He had allowed her to attend the Seasons, had permitted her to enjoy what she could, whilst dangling her future in front of her with barely concealed mirth at the power he held. Allowing her to remain as she was at present was merely his eagerness to find the very best situation for her that would benefit him.

Which was, of course, the reason that he was doing very little to help her in her attempts to join in with society and to find a match of her own. Had it not been for her dear friends, she would have barely stepped outside her father's townhouse.

"That is disappointing," her father murmured, without even a trace of such an emotion in his face, but rather, she suspected, a glimmer of delight. "Let us hope there is improvement in this situation come the morrow."

Hannah said nothing but lowered her head, praying silently that her father would soon quit the room and allow her the peace she longed for, so that she could return to her book and to her own thoughts.

"*Most* disappointing," Lord Addington stated again, turning on his heel and striding from the room, leaving Hannah to her peace again.

The door slam made her jerk with the shock of such a loud, brash sound. Picking up her book, Hannah tried to begin to read the novel again, but within moments, her vision had begun to blur as tears came into her eyes, her heart aching with a deep, terrible pain that had lingered there for such a long time. Her father cared nothing for her, wanting to use her for his own ends. She had no doubt that the gentleman her father intended her to wed would care as little for her as her father did at present. Her heart ached within her as she considered what might become of her. The last thing she wanted was to be wed to someone who cared nothing for her, but it seemed to be approaching her steadily, without any chance of escaping it. If she had even a single gentleman interested in calling upon her then she might have a smidgen of hope, but as yet, there had been none.

And then, there had been Lord Bentham.

Again came the stab of a red-hot poker piercing her heart as she thought of him. As she had helped her friend, Miss Hawkins, through what had been a difficult situation, she had found herself drawing closer to him. A viscount was an excellent prospect for her, but it was neither his title nor his fortune that drew her to him but rather his kindness and his willingness to help no matter the struggle that might face him thereafter. He had been very attentive toward her, making his evident interest clear, and Hannah had found her heart burning for him, a deep regard winding its way through her whenever they had drawn near.

But in a moment, he had gone. His attention had dried up, his presence in society had disappeared, and he had left her side without even a word of explanation. She was a fool to have even hoped for his continued regard. A vision of what awaited her rose before her eyes and Hannah closed her eyes tightly, trying to push it away from her. Tears burned in her vision and she let them fall, her shoulders shaking, her frame racked with sobs. There seemed to be no way out.

UNFORTUNATELY FOR HANNAH, being within society and at a ball did not bring any relief to her otherwise dulled spirits. She stayed near the back of the room, aware that her father had already left her alone in order to disappear into the card room, knowing full well that she could not do anything other than wait for one of her friends to find her before she could step out a little more into the ballroom.

A heavy sigh caught her chest and she closed her eyes against a sudden surge of tears. Only a few weeks ago, she had come to a ball such as this with an abundant hope springing in her heart. Lord Bentham had always been the first to greet her, eager to sign her dance card. They had enjoyed conversation and laughter, and she had found her heart filling with an affection for him that she believed had been returned. Even Miss Hawkins, her dear friend, had seen it. And now, she stood alone, mortified that she had ever thought he was truly interested in furthering his acquaintance with her.

"Miss Seymour!"

Throwing her thoughts aside, Hannah pushed away

the sadness from her face as Lady Ann approached her, a broad smile on her lips.

"Good evening, Lady Ann," she said as her friend smiled at her. "How are you?"

"Oh, very well indeed," Lady Ann replied with a bright smile. "This ball is quite magnificent, is it not?"

Hannah looked all around, seeing the many guests, hearing the wonderful music, and yet, despite it all, feeling her heart sink. "It is, yes," she said, without any true happiness in her voice. She did not quite manage to look back into Lady Ann's face, knowing that her friend could easily tell when Hannah was not speaking truthfully.

"I do hope Lord Bentham will be here this evening," Lady Ann said with a knowing smile. "He appears to be very interested in your company."

Hannah's stomach dropped, being reminded of Lord Bentham once again. Quite recently, there had been some difficulties surrounding Lord Paxton and her dear friend, Miss Hawkins, and as they had worked on sorting such things out, she had been introduced to one Lord Bentham, who had then appeared to be rather interested in furthering his acquaintance with her. However, since Lord Paxton and Miss Hawkins had become engaged, Lord Bentham had barely been seen and certainly had not sought her out as he had once done.

"You do not appear to be pleased with such a notion,

Miss Seymour," Lady Ann said quietly, her smile fading away. "Do you not enjoy his company?"

"I do indeed," Hannah replied with a quick smile. "But I will confess that I have not seen him in some weeks now. Ever since Miss Hawkins became engaged, in fact." She watched as Lady Ann frowned, but gave a small shrug of her shoulders as though to convince her friend that she did not particularly care about Lord Bentham's absence. "Let us hope that I will be able to find at least one gentleman to dance with me this evening," she finished with a small, wry smile.

"I do not understand why they do not come to seek you out," Lady Ann said with a sigh. "You are very beautiful and surely you have a good dowry?"

"I do not think such a thing matters," Hannah said sorrowfully. "Any such gentlemen take one look at my father and turn tail almost immediately." A lump stuck in her throat and she turned her gaze away from Lady Ann, not wanting to allow tears to fall despite the agony that she was in.

Lady Ann sighed heavily, one hand touching Hannah's arm for just a moment, in both sympathy and camaraderie. "Your father is something of a tyrant, I will admit," she said softly. "But surely there must be one gentleman within all of London who is not afraid to introduce himself to him?"

Hannah could not respond, knowing that her father was just as Lady Ann had described. Lord Addington was a gentleman who wielded a great deal of power. He traded in secrets, not in debts or the like, and thus, most gentlemen did not want to be even acquainted with him. Lord Addington did have *some* acquaintances, but they were the sort of gentlemen who worked with him, the sniveling, obsequious type who brought nothing good to Lord Addington's character. Thus, Hannah knew that this was the only reason that gentlemen avoided her. She could have the largest dowry in all of England, but still, gentlemen would not come to call. Her father had made sure of that.

"I am not sure what else to do," she murmured as Lady Ann sighed heavily. "My father has stated that I have this Season to find a match of my own, or else he will find someone suitable on my behalf." She threw Lady Ann a rueful look, aware of the shock on her friend's face. "I am sure that you are aware that my father has *already* decided who I am to marry, and that it will be for his own benefit."

Lady Ann lifted her chin, a sudden decisiveness in her voice and a firmness in her expression. "Then we shall do just that," she said, her hand on Hannah's arm. "I shall not allow you to be thrown to whomever your father has decided for you." Her eyes fixed to Hannah's. "What say you, Miss Seymour?"

Hannah swallowed hard. "I—I would be glad for your assistance, Lady Ann, but I fear that it will be quite impossible."

Lady Ann shook her head. "*Nothing* is impossible, Miss Seymour," she said resolutely. "You have friends around you and we will help you, I promise." She spoke of the small group of ladies with a deep bond who, together as the 'The Shadows', used their intelligence and wit to solve any puzzles or mysteries that were brought to them. Hannah had found such a bond and such a group to be a great encouragement, but lately, she had sensed herself sinking into a deep depression that she felt even her friends could not pull her from.

"You must not give up yet, Miss Seymour."

A small flicker of hope burned in Hannah's heart, but she tried to dampen it immediately, not allowing it to grow any further. "I cannot allow myself to believe it," she told her friend sorrowfully. "My dear Lady Ann, I have lost all hope."

Lady Ann's lips pursed. "Because of Lord Bentham?" she asked, and Hannah nodded miserably. "I know that you thought quite well of him and were pleased by his attentions, but surely that must bring you a little encouragement." Her eyes brightened and she smiled at Hannah, who could not find even the smallest amount of happiness to lift her mouth into a smile.

"Encouragement?"

"Yes!" Lady Ann cried, as another well-dressed young lady came to join them. "Lord Bentham was *one* gentleman who was considerate enough to show you a little attention." She shrugged. "Just because he has now withdrawn somewhat does not meant that there will not be others who can step into his place—and, in fact, do more than he."

Hannah frowned, trying to understand Lady Ann's logic, just as Lady Catherine, Lady Ann's sister, began to nod in agreement, seeming to understand their conversation without having been a part of it.

"Yes, that is quite right!" she exclaimed as Lady Ann beamed encouragingly at Hannah, all sense of doubt and worry forgotten. "You must take encouragement from it, Miss Seymour, rather than allow yourself to become despondent."

Hannah shook her head. "But my father will not change," she said slowly. "And gentlemen will still remain in fear of him, terrified that he will have some knowledge of a secret, a debt, an affair or the like, which he might use against them." She hated that her father had such a reputation, but he himself took pleasure in it, using it to revel in a sense of power that enveloped him wherever he went. A gentleman did not know when Lord Addington might pounce, demanding money or a favor of some sort in order to remain silent.

"There will be a gentleman amongst us now who has no such secrets to hide," Lady Catherine said with such a firmness that Hannah felt herself *want* to believe her. "He will be strong and determined, finding your beauty and your gentle character to be something worth his attention, no matter what might be said of your father."

She smiled warmly at Hannah, reaching out and taking her hand, as though her touch might encourage Hannah all the more. "We will have your dance card filled by the end of the evening and shall judge each gentleman carefully."

Hannah opened her mouth to protest, to say that she thought such a thing to be quite without use, but her two friends had such a look of steel in their eyes that she found her mouth closing and her head nodding in agreement.

"Good," Lady Ann said briskly, her eyes already scanning the room. "Then, let us go on our search. I am determined to see a smile on your face this evening, Miss Seymour." Her gaze darted back to Hannah, her smile both compassionate and understanding. "For you are just as worthy of happiness as the rest of us."

1

————

Viscount George Bentham shook his head to himself and groaned. He had drunk far too much last evening, and even though it was now the following evening and he was to go out to yet another social occasion, he had not quite recovered from it. Closing his eyes tightly, he rubbed at his forehead and let out another quiet groan.

"You are looking a little worse for wear."

George looked up to see Lord Paxton walking into the room. He gave his friend a slightly wry smile. "Yes, I believe so," he muttered as Lord Paxton wandered toward the fireplace and leaned on the mantelpiece, looking at George with a slightly amused look in his eyes. "In hindsight, I ought not to have celebrated my return to London in such an overt manner."

Lord Paxton shook his head. "That may well be the

case," he agreed with a smirk. "Let us hope that you do not have to return to London very often, for the sake of your head."

George grimaced and rose from his chair, glancing at his reflection in the mirror and making the tiniest adjustment to his cravat—even though he knew his valet would be deeply upset should he discover George had done so.

"Your attire is quite respectable, at least," Lord Paxton chuckled, pushing himself away from the mantlepiece and wandering toward the door. "Now, shall we depart? My dear lady is already at Lord Moncrieff's ball and I am eager to see her, I confess."

Despite his aching head, George could not help but feel a sense of contentment at the joy in his friend's eyes as he thought about Miss Hawkins. In fact, he and Lord Paxton had become friends through the situation with Lord Paxton's brother. There had been so much that Lord Paxton and Miss Hawkins had struggled through and to see them both so happy now, betrothed and looking forward to the start of their life together, made his own heart sing with joy.

"Then I shall not hold you back," he told Lord Paxton, marching toward the door with a renewed sense of determination. "And mayhap I shall find a lady of my own this Season." He chuckled as Lord Paxton looked at him with a lifted brow, questions in his eyes. "Not that I have anyone particular in mind, of course."

"No?" Lord Paxton asked with a curious look on his face, his brow still lifted. "I thought you had *some* interest in a young lady by the name of Miss Seymour."

A slight flicker of dismay crawled into George's heart and he shrugged. He could not deny that he had admired and come to think well of Miss Seymour—a lady he had become acquainted with thanks to his association with Lord Paxton—but he had not allowed himself to hold anything other than a regard for her and an admiration of her skill and intelligence. That had been all, he had told himself, well aware that there was something within himself that was holding him back.

"Come now!" Lord Paxton exclaimed, coming to a sudden stop as he turned to face George. "You cannot pretend that there was not even a flicker of interest in your heart as regards Miss Seymour. I have not mentioned her directly until this moment, thinking that you would be doing so yourself, but since you seem quite determined not to do so, I have no hesitation in bringing her up."

George winced. "I am sure I have spoken to you about my desire to remain as I am on one previous occasion at least," he said, making for the door, but Lord Paxton refused to move. "I am not ready... I..."

Lord Paxton waved a hand and made a harrumphing noise. "To state that one is not quite prepared for marriage is an excuse that many gentlemen make," he said pointedly. "I myself may have stated such a thing at one point—only to realize that to have a life filled with love is something that is more wonderful than anything else."

"But what if one does not find the love that you have found with Miss Hawkins?"

The question ricocheted out of George's mouth before he could stop himself and, immediately, heat climbed up his spine and he dropped his gaze, clearing his throat gruffly as though that would cover what he had already said.

However, it seemed that Lord Paxton did not feel such a sense of embarrassment, nor did he find George's question to be either ridiculous or foolish. Instead, he tipped his head and considered, looking toward George until, finally, George dared a look at him.

"I do believe, Lord Bentham, that one is always able to find such a thing should one be bold enough to search for it," he said, making George frown, not quite certain whether or not he agreed with this particular statement. "And it is also the desire to push aside the fears that might surround oneself when it comes to considering marriage. I am well aware of the many delights that come with being a bachelor." He chuckled a little wryly, leaving George to shake his head, knowing full well what Lord Paxton referred to. There came a freedom with being on one's own. To live a life as one chose, without any consideration for others. Perhaps, deep down, there was something in such a statement. Perhaps he did not want to let that part of his life go.

"Regardless of all that you might enjoy at present," Lord Paxton continued, as though he knew what George was thinking, "none of it is comparable to what one finds when one's heart is fully and completely filled with love for another." His smile was warm, his eyes distant and George knew at once that he was thinking of Miss Hawkins. "And their heart is filled with none but you." A small sigh escaped Lord Paxton's mouth and he gave a small shrug. "Do not let your fear of what you might have to give up hold you back."

George shifted from foot to foot, a little uncomfortable, finding himself looking at the floor rather than at his friend. If he was honest, he *was* rather afraid of what he would have to give up from his life at present. He, like so many gentlemen of the *ton*, clung to his bachelorhood with both hands, not wanting to move from it until he had no other choice but to do so. That was an extraordinary selfishness, he knew, but until he had met Miss Seymour, he had not felt any need to change such a decision.

"Come now, we will be late," Lord Paxton said, a trifle gruffly as though he were a little embarrassed to have been caught speaking so eloquently on the subject of love. "Here I am trying to quicken your pace so that I might find my dear lady quickly, only to be the one to hold you back, demanding to know how you feel about

Miss Seymour." He rolled his eyes and gave a wry smile. "Foolish, is it not?"

"Not at all," George said frankly. "I have much to think on now, it seems."

Lord Paxton did not remark on this but stepped aside and let George pass, walking out into the waiting carriage. The summer evening was warm and the sky not yet completely dark. He took in a long breath, glancing upwards for a moment. This evening, he was determined to act with all sense and consideration, refusing to imbibe more liquor than he ought. There was, he considered, a good deal for him to think about now and George intended to do just that.

"Lord Bentham."

George grinned as he accepted a glass of champagne from the footman, his eyes landing on another acquaintance, Lord Kerr. "Good evening, Lord Kerr." he exclaimed, greeting his friend with a broad smile and a firm handshake rather than the bow that would be expected for other, less intimate acquaintances. "How very good to see you again." He studied his friend closely, his lip curling just a little. "And you appear to be in fine fettle despite the plentiful whisky of last evening." From what George recalled, Lord Kerr had also enjoyed his whisky as George had done, but for whatever reason, did not seem to be even the slightest bit out of sorts.

Lord Kerr grinned, his dark blue eyes alight for a moment, a boyish grin on his face. "Mayhap that is simply because it is easier for me to pretend I am quite at my ease, when the truth is, I would much prefer to be at home, resting my poor, aching head," he said as George laughed. "Although I do hope you enjoyed last evening?" His expression turned quizzical, looking at George hopefully, as though he feared the answer would not be as he expected.

"Of course," George replied with a smile. "An excellent evening, from what I recall." Taking a satisfied breath, he turned his head to see if Lord Paxton was coming to join them, only to realize that the gentleman had already begun to make his way through the crowd of guests in search of Miss Hawkins. George allowed himself a wry smile, before turning back to speak to Lord Kerr.

"Do you expect to stay for the rest of the Season, or will you be called back to your estate again?" Lord Kerr asked, his expression rather nonchalant but a hint of interest in his voice. "After all, it was quite extraordinary the way you simply flew out of London with ne'er an explanation to anyone."

George winced and took a long sip of his champagne, taking a moment or two to consider his answer. "I hope I shall not be called back," he said slowly, not particularly wanting to labor the point. "My mother is a little unwell and required my presence. That is all."

Lord Kerr frowned, the smile fading almost immediately. "I do hope the lady is recovering?"

George nodded quickly. "Yes, she is," he answered, his heart less filled with fear than it had been before, when he had first got the summons to return to his country estate. "I admit I was a little afraid for her health, but since then, she has made such a strong recovery. She wished to travel to reside with my maiden aunt for a time and thus, I was contented to leave her to the care of my aunt's staff and to her own personal maids." He did not mention how his mother had practically brushed him aside as she strode from the house toward the carriage, stating, quite firmly, that she did not require either his help or his presence any longer. She was something of a formidable woman, so to see her back in her usual state had been quite a relief.

Lord Kerr's expression cleared. "Then I must be the first to encourage you to go forth into the ballroom and take a hold of the many delights that await you," he stated, spreading out one hand toward the ladies that were already practically filling the ballroom. "Write your name on dance cards, enjoy their company, and find yourself immersed in all that such an evening offers."

George chuckled, shaking his head. "And what if I am to consider more carefully what I am to do this

Season?" he asked his friend, not at all surprised to see the horror-struck expression on Lord Kerr's face. "You do not think it wise to consider such things?" He knew already the answer he would receive, grinning broadly as Lord Kerr put one hand to his heart.

"You know very well what my answer to such a thing would be," he told George plainly. "I will never encourage you toward matrimony, not unless you have a firm and determined reason for pursuing it."

"Such as my requirement for an heir," George said, pointedly.

Lord Kerr held up both hands, palms outwards. "That is a necessity, yes," he admitted, tilting his head just a little, "but not, perhaps, as urgent as you might consider it to be." He gestured toward George. "You are young enough yet to allow yourself *not* to consider such a thing. There will be many, *many* Seasons still to come where you might find a lady of quality with which to procure an heir, but there is no real need at present."

George let out a long breath, weighing up Lord Kerr's advice and comparing it to that of Lord Paxton's. In the middle of it, of course, sat Miss Seymour, and the knowledge that, should he allow himself, he could easily find his heart filled with the lady, as well as the urgency to remain as he was at present, unwilling to allow any change to follow him.

"You are quite correct," he heard himself say, his voice a little louder than he had intended, as though, having come to a decision, he now was encouraging himself to believe it fully. "I have nothing but my own enjoyment to consider this Season. I need not think of a wife as yet. All I need is to dance, to converse, to go to as many wonderful occasions as I can, and ensure that I do nothing other than what my heart desires." He waved a hand, dismissing Lord Paxton's previous remarks from his mind. "When the time comes for a wife, I will choose one who will provide me with decent sons, so that my family line remains strong. That is all that is required, and I certainly need not think of it yet."

"Indeed, you do not," Lord Kerr grinned, slapping George hard on the back. "Now, why do you not go out into the ballroom and find some dance cards to sign?" His eyes roved here and there, and George began to look all around himself also, taking in each young lady that stood nearby. His heart twisted painfully, feeling some sort of guilt over what he had just announced, but George ignored it with ease. Whilst he admired and respected Miss Seymour, he did not want to pursue anything serious as yet. He was not quite ready, he told himself, a glimmer of a smile on his lips. Besides which, she was bound to have a good many admirers and would not even miss his company.

Turning to look to his right and then to his left, George felt a cold hand grasp at his heart as he found himself looking straight into the eyes of Miss Seymour.

She was white-faced and tight-lipped, with a spot of red in each cheek as she looked back at him steadily. Clearly, she had overheard everything he had just said and, as he held her gaze, George felt such an overwhelming sense of shame that he had to drop his head and look away. He was mortified not only because of what he had expressed, but also because Miss Seymour had heard him say it—when only moments before, he had felt himself quite content with his decision. One look into her cool, gray eyes and George knew he had grievously injured her. He opened his mouth to apologize only to see her turning on her heel and walking away from him, weaving this way and that through the crowd, her blonde head held high. He took a stumbling step forward, thinking about pursuing her, but realized that such a venture would be quite foolish indeed. He could not be seen to be chasing after a lady, not in such an obvious manner. Closing his eyes, George forced that particular urge down, grinding it into dust before allowing himself a long, calming breath that did nothing to chase away the guilt that would not let him be.

"Are you all right, Lord Bentham?" Lord Kerr's voice was a little concerned, clearly unaware of all that had been exchanged in the look that had been shared between George and Miss Seymour. George tried to smile but his lips refused to move from the tight, thin line they had pulled themselves into. His brow remained furrowed, the light gone from his eyes entirely, but somehow, he still managed to nod.

"It is only that you *still* have not stepped out to seek a single lady's interest," Lord Kerr continued, a slight gleam in his eye. "Do you really wish to stand with me all evening?"

George forced a laugh and then strode straight ahead, leaving Lord Kerr behind. Everything seemed to be tainted now. The music clashed furiously, making him wince. The laughter of those around him sounded false, with the conversation all around him rattling noisily in his head. He could not remove the look in Miss Seymour's eyes from his mind, no matter how hard he tried, and thus, George did not stop to take anyone's name or to beg a dance from them. Instead, he made his way to the card room, picking up a brandy the moment he stepped inside and fully determined that, one way or the other, he would forget entirely about Miss Seymour and her cold, gray eyes.

2

Hannah sat forlornly in her chair, staring blindly down at the tea in her teacup and wondering just how hot it would be at present if she took a sip.

Last evening had been something of a disaster but, as yet, she had not spoken of it to a single one of her friends. Lady Ann and Lady Catherine had been in fine form, helping to fill her dance card with gentlemen willing to stand up with her but, of course, none had sought her out for a second dance, sent her flowers this morning, or expressed an intention to call upon her for afternoon tea.

Which was only made all the worse by what she had overheard coming from Lord Bentham's lips. She had seen him across the room and had made her way toward him, her feet guiding her with quick, eager steps—only to hear him speak of such selfish and egotistical desires and intentions for this coming Season that it felt as though her heart had shattered completely, the faint hope she had held for Lord Bentham being blown out at once, and the smoke it left behind mocking her furiously. The pain of it still lingered with her now.

"My lady?"

She looked up, her teacup still held in her hand. "Yes?" A footman stood in the doorway, inclining his head.

"My lady, you have four ladies seeking to call upon you," he said, and Hannah closed her eyes tightly, realizing too late that she was expecting Lady Ann, Lady Catherine, Miss Hawkins, and Lady Haddington his afternoon. She had quite forgotten.

"Yes, yes, of course," she stammered, getting to her feet and setting the teacup down on the tray, aware that she ought not to have been drinking tea if her friends were due to call. "Put them in the library, if you please. I will be along momentarily."

The footman did not say another word but stepped out into the hallway, closing the door behind him. Hannah hurried to the mirror that hung just above the fireplace, looking at her reflection and wincing at her pale cheeks and dull eyes. Pinching her cheeks until a little redness caught them, she brushed down her skirts hastily and then hurried to the door.

There is no need to speak to any of them about what is

currently pressing on your mind, she told herself firmly, refusing to allow her current distress to push itself up through her heart again. She had to keep it hidden, as she had done so many times before. The pain of knowing her father's desire to marry her off to a gentleman of his own choosing, aware of his lack of consideration for her, of his lack of care and eagerness to help her in society in any way—it had all been hidden deep within her for a very long time indeed. Hannah was well used to doing such a thing and thus fully intended to do so again.

"I do hope you had not forgotten us."

The warmth and teasing laughter in Lady Haddington's voice brought the tiniest of smiles to Hannah's face as she entered the library, looking at each of her friends in turn.

"I will confess to you that I did," she answered truthfully as the others laughed. "But I am glad to see you all here again."

The other young ladies smiled brightly and looked at each other, finding within their own hearts the same sense of contentment that had always filled Hannah's whenever they were together. There was a bond between them now, a bond that could never be broken.

"Lord Haddington calls us The Shadows," Miss Hawkins reminded everyone, as Hannah felt her heart lift a little from the swathes of sorrow that had bound it so tightly ever since last evening. "Are we to continue to refer to ourselves with that name?"

"I do not see why we should not," Lady Ann cried, clapping her hands with exuberance. "I do *so* like the name. We are, I hope, to continue seeking out certain puzzles and the like, so that we might use our wits to solve them as we have been doing thus far?"

Hannah found herself smiling at this remark. They had, as a group, managed to come to some very interesting and swift conclusions as regarded a few simpler mysteries, but there had been one or two rather difficult ones which, thankfully, they had managed to unwind completely. Prior to last evening, Hannah had every intention of continuing on with The Shadows, having allowed her heart to feel a little hope for her future, thanks to her friends' encouragements. Now, however, she felt no joy whatsoever, fearful that she would put her energy into whatever new mystery came to them rather than doing what she could to avoid the future laid out for her by her father.

"Miss Seymour?"

Lady Haddington was looking at her with concern glinting in her eyes, her expression open.

"Yes?" Hannah replied with a quick smile. "I do apologize, I was a little lost in thought."

Lady Haddington smiled in acknowledgement. "I quite understand," she said gently, gesturing toward the others. "We were wondering, given that there is very little else coming toward us, whether or not you would wish us to consider *your* situation as our next course of action?"

Hannah blinked, wondering just how much of the conversation she had missed due to her own considerations. "What do you mean?"

"Well," Lady Ann said slowly, clearly choosing her words with great care. "On the one hand, you have your father who is eager to push you toward someone he perhaps owes money to, or whom he has simply deigned worthy enough to be within his family line." She winced, not hiding the truth from Hannah, who accepted what was said without hesitation. "Then, there is the mystery surrounding Lord Bentham. Why did he disappear from London so soon after Lord Paxton announced his betrothal? I would have thought that a gentleman, so clear in his interest toward you, would have done all he could to have remained in London and pursued you properly."

This statement made Hannah crumple within, making her want to curl into a ball and hide away from her friends. They clearly were quite unaware that Lord Bentham had returned to London, else they would not have made such a remark.

"There is certainly a mystery there," Lady Catherine agreed as Miss Hawkins nodded. "Why do we not uncover the truth there, given that it would bring you a good deal of relief and might, in fact, draw you back toward each other once more?" She smiled brightly at Hannah, her eyes searching her face, but Hannah herself felt nothing but darkness clouding around her.

"I do not think that will be necessary," she said, the words sticking to her lips as she attempted to throw them out from her. "I was fortunate enough to see Lord Bentham last evening."

The gasps of astonishment, the bright smiles, and the clapping of hands suggested to Hannah that all of her friends considered this to be quite wonderful, clearly believing that there was a good deal of joy to be had in such a meeting. Her heart ached as she tried to find a way to explain the truth of what had occurred.

"It was not a welcome meeting," she continued somberly, aware of how their faces all dropped, the smiles vanishing in a moment. "I went to approach Lord Bentham, to greet him and express my joy at seeing him again, only to overhear him speaking with such openness and honesty that I feel as though I am only now seeing him for the very first time."

Lady Ann blinked in confusion, glancing around at the others before she spoke. "What do you mean?" she asked softly, and Hannah shook her head and sighed. "What was it that he said that brought you such sorrow?"

Hating the pain that burned in her as she tried to explain, Hannah took in a shuddering breath, fighting to keep her emotions under control. "He was in the middle of a short speech to his acquaintance as regarded his intentions for the Season," she said, a little darkly. "It is all to be nothing more than a few more weeks of enjoyment for him, doing as he pleases and thinking nothing of his own future. There is to be no serious consideration of a wife or even courtship. Thus," she finished, her voice catching, "I must consider that his prior interest in me was nothing more than a vague fascination on his part, which has now entirely ended."

For a few minutes, there came nothing but silence. Hannah did not remove her gaze from where it had fixed itself, looking resolutely at one of the shelves of books without having the least flicker of interest in what any of the titles were. She dared not look at her friends, hating that there would be a good deal of sympathy on each of their faces—something she did not want to see from any of them given just how raw her own emotions were at present.

"Well, I, for one, am utterly astonished at such behavior."

It was not Lady Ann or Lady Catherine who spoke first, as Hannah might have expected, given their somewhat outspoken natures. Rather, it was Miss Hawkins, who knew precisely just how close Hannah and Lord Bentham had become over the last few weeks. Her face was red, her eyes blazing with an anger Hannah had never seen before, and her hands were in tight fists as she glared at Hannah as though she were the one at fault.

"And after all that you have shared with him, too," Miss Hawkins continued, her voice loud and filling the room. "He is not the gentleman I thought him to be. I am utterly astonished and very disappointed indeed."

"As am I," Lady Haddington stated firmly. "That is disgraceful behavior on his part, Miss Seymour. I do hope you are not too distraught."

Hannah, who was a little overcome by Miss Hawkins' furious reaction, could only murmur something incomprehensible. She looked at Lady Ann and Lady Catherine, who both were wearing similar expressions of dismay, their eyes glinting with a hint of resentment toward Lord Bentham. "I—I will not pretend I have not been greatly upset by what I overheard," she stammered as Lady Haddington rose from her chair and began to pace up and down the room in what was perhaps a futile attempt to rid herself of all that she felt. "Lord Bentham is aware that I overheard him but we did not exchange any words thereafter."

"Then we will continue on as we have been before," Lady Ann said with a dramatic flourish, her hair bouncing around as she lifted her chin. "We will make every attempt to find you a suitable gentleman, who will not do as Lord Bentham has done." Her lips thinned, her eyes sparkling with anger over what Hannah had endured. "You will be rescued from your father's intentions one way or the other."

Hannah, who had not yet explained to Lady Haddington what her father had said, was then forced to recount what he had stated, seeing how her eyes flared with horror and disgust that a gentleman would treat his daughter in such a manner.

"Then I must concur with Lady Ann," Lady Haddington said briskly. "We will find you a much more suitable gentleman in the next few weeks, Miss Seymour. And if your father makes to do as he has threatened, then I shall take you to the Haddington estate and insist that you reside there temporarily, so that we have a little more time to ensure you are not wed to some odious gentleman who cares nothing for you." She spoke with such fervency and determination that Hannah found herself smiling, her eyes brimming with tears as a flurry of hope began to push aside all the pain and sorrow that had engulfed her only a short time ago. She felt quite weary all of a sudden, aware that her feelings had changed rapidly from one emotion to the next, but looking around at her friends, Hannah felt herself encouraged, seeing the resoluteness in each of their faces and knowing that their true friendship brought her both happiness and relief.

"I thank you," she said sincerely, as Lady Haddington smiled warmly. "I do not know what else to say than that."

Miss Hawkins did not quite manage to smile, her anger still clearly visible in her expression, but when she spoke, her voice was soft.

"You need not say anything," she said gently. "We are glad to come alongside you."

"Although," Lady Catherine added with a glimmer of mirth in her eye, "let us hope that we do not have any other mysteries thrown at us for the present, so that we might focus all of our intentions on you."

Hannah laughed and made to respond, only for the library door to fly open and a young lady to stumble inside. Her hair was askew, her face pale and her eyes wide with fright.

"I do apologize, my lady," cried the butler, hurrying inside after the lady. "I do not know where this young lady came from. She just appeared at the front door and asked where you were. When I answered her, she flew through the house, searching each room before she found you." He reached out for the young lady but did not quite touch her, pulling his hand back in evident fear that he ought not to do so. This was, Hannah realized, the reason that the lady had been able to search from room to room without any sort of impediment.

"Please," the young lady cried, her eyes darting from one person to the next, her chest rising and falling rapidly as she gulped in air. "Please, you must hide me!"

Hannah stared at the young lady in astonishment,

her heart quickening as the lady reached out one hand toward her, as though begging her for her help.

"I have nowhere else to go," the young lady pleaded, her tears falling to her cheeks like the rain on a spring morning. "I must stay here. My uncle does not know I have gone, for I left before he had risen. I took nothing with me, but I beg you for your help. You are The Shadows, are you not?" She did not wait for them to answer but continued to speak with great urgency. "Then I must beg you for your aid, for I am in a great tangle and must find a way to escape it."

"We are The Shadows, yes," Lady Haddington said as Hannah rose to her feet, aware of the astonishment that swept around her. She drew near the young lady, taking her closer to the fireplace and gesturing for her to sit down, before going to speak quietly to the butler. "What is it that you want from us?"

The butler, having been duly informed to keep the arrival of this young lady from the rest of the staff and, in particular, from Hannah's father, scurried off to fetch another tea tray and some sustenance for the as yet unidentified lady. Hannah turned around to look at the stranger a little more closely, choosing not to seat herself again.

"I want you to hide me," the lady whispered, her eyes still huge in her face, her cheeks whiter than even a few minutes before. "Do you not understand? I must escape. I must go to her."

Hannah swallowed hard, her brows lowering as she saw Lady Catherine dart a glance up toward her, realizing that what the lady spoke of made very little sense but that she also appeared to be deeply upset and very afraid.

"Might I enquire as to your name?" Lady Ann asked quietly. "You appear to be in great distress, and I am sure we would be glad to help you." Quickly, she introduced the other ladies to their guest, before waiting for her to speak.

The lady sniffed and rubbed her nose in an indelicate fashion. "I am Miss Sarah Lewisham," she said, without anyone having a spark of recognition as to who she might be. "My uncle is Lord Greene. My mother is alive but does not live with my uncle, but rather resides in the Dower house, which he has granted to her."

"That is kind of him," Lady Catherine remarked, only for Miss Lewisham to shake her head and begin to cry in earnest. Apparently, this was not a kindness, for the lady was deeply upset indeed.

"Is she in London with you?" Hannah asked, and Miss Lewisham shook her head. "Then it is just you and your uncle present in London for the Season?"

Miss Lewisham pulled out what appeared to be an already damp handkerchief and pressed it to her eyes, stemming the flow of tears for a few moments. "It is," she sniffed, although her words were barely audible, such was the rasping of her voice. "And I have already suffered for it."

Hannah frowned, seeing the flicker of fear that crossed Miss Lewisham's face and finding herself to be a little wary of this unknown uncle, wondering what it was that he had done that was making Miss Lewisham so distraught.

"What trouble is it that you speak of?" she asked, as gently as she could. "Are you to be wed to someone that you have no knowledge of?" She found herself wincing inwardly at such a remark but knew full well that it was the plight of many a young lady who came to London.

Miss Lewisham shook her head, her fingers twisting together in her lap. "My mother has stated that there has long been an arrangement between myself and a very worthy gentleman," she said hoarsely. "I have not even met the gentleman, having been ensconced in my uncle's estate." She swallowed hard and closed her eyes tightly, shuddering with the effort of speaking. "My father passed away some years ago and I have had a prolonged mourning period, put in place by my uncle. Whilst going through my father's papers, the solicitors discovered that a betrothal agreement has been arranged for me—although it was only to take place if my father passed away." Opening her eyes, she let out a long breath. "I did not know my father had arranged for such a thing. No plans for our marriage have been made as yet and I confess that I have never met the gentleman in question."

"Oh!" Lady Haddington exclaimed in surprise. "And the gentleman has not expressed concern or sought to seek you out, knowing now that your father has passed?"

Miss Lewisham sniffed and lifted her arms in a gesture of hopelessness. "I do not really know why but it appears that he cares nothing for the arrangement. I thought myself free, but my uncle insists that this arrangement will stand, and has come to London to speak to this gentleman to demand that it continue as planned."

"And this, I presume, is not because your uncle truly cares for you?" Miss Hawkins asked sympathetically, and Miss Lewisham nodded sadly. "There is some other reason?"

Sniffing, Miss Lewisham wiped her eyes. "It is worse than you might think, Miss Hawkins," she whispered brokenly. "He has demanded that I obey him and due to the fear that lingers in my heart because of him, I cannot turn away." Her head lowered and her shoulders slumped. "My mother has not stood by my side as I have hoped. She has gone to the Dower house and resides there, far away from me."

Hannah's frown deepened, her brows tugging together as she glanced from one lady to the next. The Shadows were all watching Miss Lewisham with expressions ranging from concern to interested anticipation.

"We will not think badly of you, Miss Lewisham," Hannah said gently, wanting to reassure the lady. "You have come here for help, have you not?" She smiled kindly. "Tell us what your uncle has told you to do."

Miss Lewisham drew in a shaking breath, closing her eyes tightly for a moment. "My uncle is searching for a set of two small, identical ornaments," she told the group. "One was given to the father of the gentleman I am to marry, at the time of the agreement. I was given the other." A slightly wistful smile came over her face. "My father always brought it to my attention, reminding me to take good care of it. I did not know why, of course, for I was only a small child, but it became dear to me because of my father's insistence that it was important."

"It was a symbol, I suppose," Lady Catherine murmured, looking around the room. "When the time came, the ornaments would be brought back together again, when the two family lines joined."

Miss Lewisham nodded. "Yes, that is it precisely," she agreed.

"Might I ask why your uncle has not merely asked this gentleman for the return of the ornament?" Hannah asked as a flicker of a frown crossed Miss Lewisham's face. "Why did he not simply seek to have it returned, given that the betrothal has not led to marriage?"

Miss Lewisham hesitated, then shook her head. "I

do not know. My uncle states that there is a clause that states that the ornament remains with my betrothed if there is no marriage, but he has not shown it to me."

"I see," Hannah murmured, still not truly understanding. "Then, since the arrangement has lapsed and the gentleman in question has not pursued your marriage or compensation for the fact that it has *not* occurred, then the ornament remains with his family."

Nodding, Miss Lewisham lips quivered.

"And your uncle wishes you to retrieve it somehow. Might I ask what it is?"

Again, Miss Lewisham's eyes filled with tears. "My family has the gentleman figurine, so I expect that he holds the lady. It is a symbol of our engagement and subsequent marriage," she said hoarsely. "But no doubt, it will be at the gentleman's estate and the only way I shall *ever* manage to visit there is if I am brought there as his wife. My uncle states that the figurine is only to be given to me after the marriage has taken place." A sob caught in her throat and she looked down at the ground, her eyes brimming. "I do not know what else I shall do. My uncle has refused to allow me to depart the house, insisting that I accompany him to certain social occasions but never stepping out of his sight." She swallowed hard. "It was only by chance that I heard of you and managed to find out a name or two. I have run from my uncle's house in desperate need of your help, for unless I continue with this engagement without question, unless I marry and procure this ornament, then I shall never see my mother again."

Hannah's stomach dropped and she stared at Miss Lewisham, seeing how tears fell onto her cheeks, forming little rivers until they fell to the floor in small droplets. The lady's shoulders shook hard and Hannah moved forward at once, putting one arm around Miss Lewisham and shaking her head in horror.

"Your mother is being *kept* at the Dower house, rather than merely enjoying a quiet stay there?" she asked with concern, and Miss Lewisham nodded, unable to form a single word through her sobs. "You have been separated from her?"

"I have," Miss Lewisham cried, her voice barely audible, such was the sound of her sobs. "She and I only have each other. My brother died in infancy and the loss of my father quite broke my mother's heart. To have her placed in the Dower house, never to be allowed to depart from it—for the staff are her guards—has quite torn us asunder. And I do not know what else I can do other than to obey my uncle."

Hannah shook her head again, feeling anger swell in her chest. "We will help you, Miss Lewisham," she said firmly. "You need not fear."

"Of course we will," Lady Haddington agreed kindly. "You are not alone in this any longer, Miss Lewisham."

Miss Lewisham pressed her hands to her eyes. "I

cannot thank you enough," she whispered, her voice shaking with emotion. "You are all very kind."

Hannah kept her hand tightly on the lady's shoulder. "Now, you must tell us the name of this gentleman you are betrothed to," she said, wondering if anyone would know of him. "The one your uncle is to speak to, in order to insist that the arrangement goes ahead."

Nodding, Miss Lewisham wiped her eyes and dropped her hands, although Hannah was glad to see that she did not appear as pale as before.

"He is a gentleman I have not yet met," she said with a small shrug. "A viscount, I believe."

"There are plenty of those in London," Miss Hawkins laughed, the tension easing for a moment.

"Indeed." Miss Lewisham's smile was minute, but it was still very much present. "He is Viscount Bentham, I think. He has an estate far from London, but a town-house here, of course." She closed her eyes tightly and Hannah felt a shudder run through her frame. "I cannot tell whether the ornament is in London or at his estate, but I would presume—"

"Viscount Bentham?"

To her own ears, Hannah heard her voice thin and wispy, barely able to hold any strength. Her hand slipped from Miss Lewisham's shoulder and she heard Miss Hawkins take in a quick breath, clearly fully aware of the shock that now rifled through Hannah's frame.

"Yes, that is what I said," Miss Lewisham answered

sorrowfully. "Pray, do you know of him? Is he a very cruel gentleman?"

Hannah found herself shaking her head, not quite sure what she ought to say. Was this the reason for Lord Bentham's withdrawal from society? Had he shown her attention in the hope that she might be open to his advances, even though he clearly had no intention of pursuing anything else with her? She backed away slowly from Miss Lewisham, finding herself being guided to a chair by one of her friends.

"No," she whispered as she sank down into a chair. "No, he is not a cruel gentleman by any means." Her eyes stared unseeingly at Miss Lewisham. "At least, I did not think he was until this very moment."

3

———

"My lord, you have a visitor."

George stood up at once, fully expecting it to be Lord Kerr come to call. After they had enjoyed a very good evening some two days ago, he had arranged to call, but he was now a little overdue.

"Very good," he said, gesturing to his butler to open the door. "Show him in at once."

The butler hesitated for just a moment but then stepped away, making George frown. His staff normally did as he asked without even a momentary pause, so for the butler to stop as he had done was something of a surprise. Had something happened to Lord Kerr?

"Lord Greene," the butler intoned as a gentleman that George had never met before in his life stepped into the room. He did not bow but merely inclined his head, whilst keeping his icy gaze trained on George.

Recovering himself a little, George cleared his throat and bowed, choosing to behave respectfully even if Lord Greene did not.

"No refreshments, Taylor," he told his butler as he withdrew, making it quite clear to his guest that he was not about to be granted any sort of welcome given his strange and unexpected arrival at George's house. A gentleman did not simply appear, unexpected and unwelcome, at another man's home and expect to be graciously welcomed.

"I do hope you will not treat my niece this way when she is your wife."

George narrowed his eyes, although there came an uncomfortable stirring in his stomach at this remark which he did not permit to be shown in his expression.

"I do not believe we are introduced, sir," he said pointedly. "Nor did I receive a note from you begging an audience." He ignored the gentleman's remark entirely and merely arched an eyebrow, looking at the man with a firm eye. His visitor was a tall man with broad shoulders but a rather round middle. With dark hair sparked with silver and a thick, gray moustache, which did not detract from his weak chin, George considered him to be a man in his later years, although certainly with a good deal of life left in him still. He had been introduced as Lord Greene, which meant that he certainly had a title, and from the cut of his clothes, George could tell that there was a good deal of refinement about him. He would have expected a gentleman of the *ton* to know what was expected in matters such as these, and certainly was not about to extend any sort of friendship to someone who had been so rude.

"Surely you were expecting me," the gentleman remarked coolly, folding himself slowly into a chair without even having been invited. "Or can it be that you did not hear of my brother's death?" He eyed George carefully, as though he believed now that George was busy telling untruths, which left George all the more confused. "Perhaps that is why you did not attend his funeral."

"I do not believe I have ever met you before," George stated firmly, "nor was I ever acquainted with your brother, from whom, I presume, you inherited the title."

"You presume correctly," Lord Greene replied with a sharp look in his eye. "I was rather surprised that you did not come to pay your respects, what with all that has been shared between you."

George threw up his hands. "Until you begin to start speaking sense, I can share no understanding with you as regards what you are speaking of," he said, growing rather angry with the gentleman's manner toward him. "Now, unless you begin to speak clearly, I will have to ask you to depart from my house." He rose from his chair and gestured toward the door, only for Lord

Greene to smile indolently at him. Rage began to burn in his heart, and he was about to go and shout for his butler to drag Lord Greene from the house, but Lord Greene waved a hand, gesturing for George to sit back in his chair.

His ire burned all the hotter and George glared at the fellow, his hands curling into fists as he stood exactly where he was, refusing to do as the gentleman expected. He was not about to be ordered around in his own house.

"I do not understand why you pretend so," Lord Greene said softly, his green eyes glittering malevolently at George, whose jaw worked furiously as he tried to keep his temper. "However, since it appears that you will not admit to knowing what I speak of, I shall indulge you." He cleared his throat and George felt as though he were on the edge of a precipice, swaying forward and back.

"You are betrothed," Lord Greene said calmly, as though George ought to know what he was about to say. "My niece, Miss Amelia Lewisham, is your intended bride."

George stared at the man, wondering if there was something wrong with his intellect. He had never once made any sort of arrangement with the lady, had never once agreed to his betrothal to anyone. Lord Greene must be mistaken.

"I believe this betrothal was agreed upon by your

respective fathers," Lord Greene continued with a small shrug. "I will be quite truthful with you, however." He cleared his throat, looking at George with a sharp eye. "The papers we have lack the late Lord Bentham's seal, but it does have his signature." Another glitter entered his eyes. "They possess Miss Lewisham's late father's signature and seal, however. I am quite certain that you will have copies of your own which *will* have the seal, confirming that it was your father's wish that you marry Miss Lewisham on the event of her father's death." He grimaced, whilst George let out a long breath, his chest tight. "She *was* to be wed to you within a few months of her mourning period coming to an end, which, of course, has now passed. However, given that I was not aware of such an arrangement, I expect that you will be willing to continue with the arrangement as planned, even if it takes place a little later than the agreement stated."

Silence met his words as George stared blankly at him. He could hear nothing but the sound of his own rasping breaths, trying to work out whether what this gentleman said could be true. His mind began to chew slowly over what had been said, his thoughts centering on one thing—had his father ever mentioned such an arrangement?

"You will find the papers, I am sure," Lord Greene said, his voice breaking open the silence, shattering the quiet around them. "I could show you the ones we have, if you would be glad of them."

"I—I would," George stammered, his voice shuddering out of him. "I cannot believe that there is any sort of betrothal between myself and your niece. My father never once spoke of it."

Lord Greene arched his eyebrow, looking at him lazily. "I see," he said without any sort of conviction in his voice. "Then I would be glad to bring them to you without delay."

George found himself nodding, wondering if he would have to write to his mother to see if she knew of any such thing.

"Then I will return on the morrow to bring you these papers," Lord Greene said, starting to rise from his chair. "I do now feel inclined to believe that you do not know anything of what I speak, but that does not mean that the agreement is forgotten. Given that my niece has had to deal with the death of her father and the subsequent mourning period which meant that she could not wed even if she wished to, I would presume that you would not insist that the agreement in itself is void."

"Of course not," George mumbled, only to realize what he had said. Attempting to stammer that he did not mean any such thing, that there was certainly to be a good deal more discussion before he accepted any such agreement, he soon realized it was much too late, as Lord Greene rose, strode to the door, and thanked him loudly for his acceptance of what had just been said. George was left standing quietly, his mouth a little ajar and his feet frozen to the floor as the door closed tightly on Lord Greene.

He could not think of what to do next. His thoughts were spiraling in all directions, his mouth dry as he sank down into a chair, looking at the tapestry hanging from the wall as though it would give him some answers.

Betrothed? He could not be betrothed to someone he did not know. His father would have mentioned something of it to him, surely?

But your father died suddenly, without any warning, said a quiet voice in his head. *Perhaps he had always intended to but could not do so.*

Closing his eyes, George put his head in his hands, aware that the groaning he heard came from his own lips. This was quite impossible. He could not find himself suddenly engaged to a lady he had never once met. Of course, such agreements were made very often, but they were always spoken of between those involved. Such an arrangement must have been made when he was very young, unable to respond or recall anything in any way. Perhaps in the grief and the sorrow that had followed his father's death, when he himself had to take on the title long before he was truly prepared to do so, his mother had quite forgotten about it all and thus had not mentioned it to him either. He would have to write to her at once, to find out whether she knew of such a thing.

"Lord Paxton, my lord," the butler announced.

George looked up with weary eyes, seeing his friend stride into the room, an overly bright smile on his face.

"Lord Paxton," he muttered, rubbing a hand over his eyes. "I was not expecting you."

Lord Paxton chuckled and threw himself into a chair, eyeing George with a knowing look in his eyes. "You have been enjoying yourself again, I presume?"

George shook his head, half wishing he had done so. "I have not," he answered truthfully. "My head is quite clear."

"Then why do you look the worse for wear?" Lord Paxton asked with another chuckle. "You need not pretend."

Grimacing, George let out another long breath, not quite certain what to say. He could not tell Lord Paxton what Lord Greene had said, he decided, without having any real proof about it all. His head was much too full, his thoughts still too tangled for him to speak.

"I think I may have to return to my estate," he mumbled, knowing that there would be no documents or the like here in London. His father had kept everything within the estate. George frowned, realizing that, in all of the years he had been viscount, he had never once found anything relating to his supposed engagement. Had his father hidden it somewhere? Or was this all a ruse on Lord Greene's part? Would there be some sort of reason for such a deception? He simply could not—

"Lord Bentham?"

George looked up, seeing Lord Paxton's curious expression. His thoughts had clearly shown on his face and he cleared his throat, a little embarrassed.

"My apologies," he said, wondering how to express himself clearly but without giving his confusion away. "Yes, as I was saying, I think I must return to my estate."

Lord Paxton looked a little surprised. "A house party?" he asked. "I did not think you had such a thing planned."

"It is not a—"

"I would be glad to help you," Lord Paxton continued, sounding quite eager. "A house party before my marriage to Miss Hawkins would be just the thing."

George opened his mouth to protest, to say that he could not have a house party and had no intention of doing so, but for whatever reason, Lord Paxton was already filled with ideas, striding around the room and gesticulating furiously.

"You should invite a good few guests, of course," Lord Paxton continued. "You will *have* to invite Miss Hawkins' companions, of course—Lady Catherine and Lady Ann and their mother, mayhap. Then, of course, Miss Seymour and her..." He frowned. "Her father will not come, of course, but I am sure he would permit her to attend with Miss Hawkins. They are very dear friends." His frown lifted and he smiled broadly, whilst George felt himself sink lower and lower into his seat. "Lord and Lady Haddington, as well."

"You want me to invite The Shadows," George interrupted dully. "They need respite after the troubles you and Miss Hawkins faced, I presume."

Lord Paxton waved a hand. "Something like that," he said, his tone noncommittal. "There are a few others, of course, that I would recommend, but I am sure they will all be able to attend, even if it is a rather hasty invitation." He shrugged and dropped into a chair. "There are only a few weeks left of the Season, however. I am sure everyone will be very glad to come."

George blinked, not quite sure what to say. He wanted to say that he could not have a house party, but there was far too much on his mind for him to form any comprehensible explanation. For a moment, he had the brief thought that if he *was* to find himself betrothed, a house party might be an excellent situation for him to meet his bride.

"When would you wish to have the invitations sent out?" Lord Paxton asked, as though the entire thing had been already agreed upon. "The staff will need time to prepare for your house party, of course, but a week or so should be enough, especially since you have some staff here in London, able to bring whatever you require from here to there."

"Perhaps a fortnight," George muttered, aware now that he was to have a house party and could no longer step back from it. "I should have the house and the staff prepared by then."

Lord Paxton clapped his hands together and beamed. "And for how long?"

"A good few days," George replied with a sigh, no smile lifting his own features. "It is an excellent time for hunting and shooting, of course."

"Capital!" Lord Paxton boomed, clearly quite delighted. "Mayhap The Shadows and I could come a few days earlier, in order to help with all the arrangements."

George shrugged, already resigned to this house party now actually happening. "I suppose that would be beneficial."

"Excellent!" Lord Paxton rose from his chair and hurried toward the door. "I shall tell Miss Hawkins and the other Shadows at once, so that they know to prepare for the invitation. Until this evening, Lord Bentham."

George opened his mouth to bid his friend farewell, only for the words to stay within as the door shut behind him. He felt nothing but a sinking of his heart and a deep, wrenching disbelief that rattled right through him. Was this really true? Was he to throw this house party in order to meet his betrothed? He could not quite believe it, feeling a terrible ache deep within his heart as he sighed heavily.

And then, he thought of Miss Seymour. Thinking of her made his heart slice with pain, forcing him to catch his breath. He had not expected to even consider her under his present circumstances, but now, as he realized he might find himself soon married to a lady he did not even know, he felt a deep, shattering agony that seared his mind. If he had chosen to pursue Miss Seymour, he might now find himself engaged and would have been able to shun Lord Greene's request and state that the betrothal agreement was entirely void, given that Miss Lewisham was now past the agreed age for their marriage to take place.

"Stop ruminating," he told himself aloud, lifting his head and drawing in a long breath, filling his chest and spreading his arms out wide, as though to shake off his distress. "The papers may turn out to be quite false. There may be nothing there at all. And all of this will be for nothing."

And if that is the case, he told himself, rising to his feet and making for the door, *then I shall, mayhap, consider Miss Seymour again. Perhaps I have been foolish there.*

With such a thought ringing in his mind, George rushed to his study, determined to start making arrangements for his house party at once. He would also have to go to his solicitors almost at once, to make quite certain that no such papers had been filed by his father.

Thereafter, he could do nothing but wait for Lord Greene to return, feeling as though the man held both his fate and his future in his hands. A trickle of sweat ran down his neck and he pulled a handkerchief from his pocket, wiping it away as quickly as he could. How odd it was to find himself so distracted, so confused and upset, when only a few hours ago he had found himself delighted with how the Season was progressing, thinking that there was nothing more he enjoyed than spending time in London. Stepping into the study, George made for the table in the corner, picking up a glass and filling it with brandy. Throwing it back, he swallowed it quickly, letting the warmth of the brandy run through him, restoring him a little. Letting out his breath slowly, he set the glass down and walked to his desk, ready to prepare a list of guests. It was not what he had thought he would be doing nor what he wished to do, but fate had grasped at him and would not let him go. He was bound to his next course of action and could not turn from it now, no matter what happened.

4

<hr>

Holding the invitation in her hand, Hannah looked down at it and tried to force her tears back from her eyes. She did not want to cry, did not want to allow any sort of upset to appear in her expression, and yet it was with a great pain in her heart that she approached her father's study.

"You find this very difficult, I know."

Hannah swallowed hard and looked across at Miss Hawkins, who had completely refused to remain anywhere other than by Hannah's side.

"How can I not?" she asked hoarsely, her vision blurring as she looked at her invitation again, seeing Lord Bentham's name written there. "I thought he was interested in furthering an acquaintance with me and now..." She shook her head, her throat constricting.

"Courage, my dear friend," Miss Hawkins answered

gently, her hand looping through Hannah's arm. "I cannot allow you to refuse the invitation and remain at home."

"But I can see no reason to attend," Hannah protested weakly, her heart in pieces on the floor, just as it had been when she had first heard Lord Bentham's name being spoken by Miss Lewisham. She did not understand how he could have spoken so selfishly about his need to live as he wished for some time, refusing to consider a bride or the like, only to find out that he was now betrothed to Miss Lewisham. "There is no need for my presence. The Shadows will do very well without me."

Miss Hawkins shook her head. "You may think so, but I am certain that we require your intelligence and your gentle heart," she answered as they came to a stop just a few paces away from Lord Addington's study. "Besides which, I cannot, in good conscience, allow you to remain here alone."

Hannah made to protest but knew there was nothing for her to say. Her friends had all insisted that she attend with them, promising her that there were still opportunities for her to find a suitable match, even at the house party. Even if it was *not* to be Lord Bentham. She did not believe them, knowing that her father's ominous reputation would still overshadow her no matter where she went. Yet there was a part of her that did not want to linger in London whilst the rest of The Shadows went to

Lord Bentham's estate, even though the last person she wished to be with was Lord Bentham himself.

"Very well," she whispered, her eyes fixed on the door in front of her as she took in a deep breath, walking forward with Miss Hawkins by her side. Knocking gently, she waited for the gruff call to come, before pushing the door open and stepping inside.

"Lord Addington," Miss Hawkins said immediately, her voice melodious and bright. "Good afternoon."

Tension filled Hannah as she drew closer to her father, aware that he had not risen to greet Miss Hawkins, even though propriety stated he ought to do so. Her father was looking at her from under dark brows, his mouth in a thin line, as though he knew she was coming to ask for something he did not want to grant her.

"I have received an invitation to a house party, Father," she began, hating how weak her voice sounded. "Miss Hawkins has also been invited and has suggested that I–"

"I know that you are *very* busy with matters here in London," Miss Hawkins interrupted, her voice filling the room. "I would be glad to take Miss Seymour with me, and will furnish her with a lady's maid, if you cannot spare one." She smiled at Lord Addington, but Hannah could not do so, a slight tremor running up her spine as she watched her father, seeing how he looked at Miss Hawkins with something akin to anger in his eyes. Did he feel as though Hannah had constructed this particular situation, so that he would have no other choice but to agree?

"You think a house party is the answer to your particular difficulties at present, Hannah?"

Lord Addington's voice did not hold any sort of kindness, but rather a scornful disregard that held nothing but mockery. One eyebrow lifted, his lip curling upwards.

"I—I have until the end of the Season, Father," Hannah reminded him, her voice still wavering as she forced the words from her mouth. "The house party might be—"

"You are ungrateful," her father interrupted, the words spat from his mouth. "I have someone in mind for you who would be more than acceptable, were you not so stubborn." He waved a hand toward her. "I have only granted you until the end of the Season so that you cannot spend the rest of your days complaining that you were not given any opportunity to find a husband of your own."

Hannah knew this was not the case but did not shake her head in disagreement. Her father cared very little for her. This arrangement he intended for her would bring him a boon of some sort and he had not allowed her an opportunity in order to prevent her complaining, but no doubt only to secure the best arrangement he could manage from whomever it was that wanted her hand in marriage. On top of which, Hannah knew that he liked to wield his power over her with such force that it would bring her nothing but suffering and fear. As much as she wanted to stand up to him, to prevent this from affecting her in any way, she battled against her sorrow and trepidation more and more as her father's power grew.

"Then surely," she said, as Miss Hawkins' hand tightened on her arm, encouraging her just a little, "you can permit me this final opportunity, Father."

He snorted. "Little good it will do you."

Pressing her lips together, Hannah held her breath, looking at the floor rather than at her father. If he refused her, then she could not attend, for if she went without his permission, then her reputation would be damaged—and she was quite certain that he would ride out after her and drag her back to London for an almost immediate marriage to whomever he had chosen.

"As I have said, Lord Addington," Miss Hawkins said, breaking the silence, "Miss Seymour will be quite safe within the care of myself and my own family. There is nothing that you need concern yourself with."

Lord Addington snorted again and looked up toward Hannah, who held her breath, finding it difficult to hold his gaze—but hold it she did, although it seemed to take every fiber of her being to do so.

Lord Addington sighed, sat back, and waved a hand. "Very well," he grunted, making Hannah start with surprise and relief. "But have no doubt, daughter, your betrothed will be waiting for you when you return."

Her happiness evaporated in a moment and she dropped her head, seeing the dark smile on her father's face.

"I thank you, Lord Addington," Miss Hawkins said, turning Hannah gently. "Do forgive us for interrupting you."

Hannah felt herself being led out of the room by her friend, her heart sinking all the more into her shoes as she heard the door being shut behind her, clanging noisily along the hallway.

"Well," Miss Hawkins said brightly, "I am sure that there is something of a happiness within your heart."

"How can there be?" Hannah said bitterly. "I will return from the house party as I go—alone and with a dark cloud over me. I will not find a suitable gentleman. I will—"

"You will go to Lady Haddington's," Miss Hawkins said briskly. "If the house party comes to an end and you are still without a match, then to Lady Haddington's you shall go." She smiled brightly, steel glinting in her eyes. "I know there is nothing that your father can have on Lord Haddington that would cause him to show any sort of fear toward him."

Hannah swallowed her tears, her throat aching with the strain of keeping her emotions under control. They walked back toward the drawing room together and

Hannah found she could not speak, such was the pain in her heart.

"It may damage your reputation somewhat," Miss Hawkins continued practically, "but we *will* find you someone kind, with a good character, Miss Seymour. You are not under your father's control."

Shaking her head, Hannah wanted to tell her friend that yes, she *was* under her father's control and that she had always been so, but the words would not leave her mouth. With Miss Hawkins still guiding her, they walked into the drawing room, and Miss Hawkins sat her down before ringing the bell, knowing the tea would be brought.

"This is a good opportunity," Miss Hawkins continued, coming to sit beside her friend. "Lord Paxton did excellently when it came to convincing Lord Bentham to have a house party—although I am not quite certain how he did it." She laughed softly and Hannah could not help but smile, feeling a little better now that she had finished her discussion with her father. "We will find the truth, Miss Seymour, I am sure of it."

Hannah nodded but closed her eyes. "And is Lord Bentham to invite Miss Lewisham?" she asked, her voice barely loud enough for Miss Hawkins to hear. "He will, of course, given that she is his betrothed?"

Miss Hawkins frowned. "We are not quite certain if the betrothal stands," she reminded Hannah. "Obviously, Lord Paxton could not mention it, given that it is not something he is meant to have knowledge of. But, in time, I am sure that Lord Bentham will speak to Lord Paxton of what has occurred and mayhap, then, we can know the truth."

"And perhaps ask him about this strange ornament," Hannah murmured quietly, rubbing her hand over her eyes. "I will not pretend that my heart is in this particular puzzle, Miss Hawkins. I have so much confusion, so much upset deep within my heart, but I will do what I can, no matter what."

Miss Hawkins pressed her hand and looked into Hannah's eyes, that determination that had become a part of her character now evident with her expression. "You will find happiness, Miss Seymour," she said firmly. "No matter what you may face, you will not always be as you are at present. I am quite sure of that."

Be bold.

Hannah swallowed hard as she walked into the evening's soiree held at none other than Lord Greene's townhouse, having received an invitation from Miss Lewisham herself. After they had calmed Miss Lewisham down, The Shadows had managed to come up with a plan that had not only reassured Miss Lewisham but had given them an opportunity to find out what these ornaments meant. Lord Paxton had managed to do as he had been asked, securing a house party at Lord Bentham's home despite the host's evident shock and surprise that such a thing was to occur.

Miss Lewisham had been encouraged to return to her uncle's home and had, in the end, been convinced to do so. She had clearly managed to achieve her only goal, which was to convince her uncle to have a small soiree which she could invite The Shadows to. Given that Miss Lewisham was unable to step outside her townhouse without her uncle by her side, this was the only chance they would have to talk about what was to happen next.

"Ah, good evening, Miss Seymour."

"Miss Lewisham." Hannah curtsied beautifully, finding it quite difficult to look the lady in the face, feeling a sense of awkwardness fill her. Miss Lewisham had no knowledge of what had occurred between Hannah and Lord Bentham and, as such, did not display any discomfort whatsoever.

"I am very glad to see you," Miss Lewisham said breathlessly, looking quite different from the windswept, tearful lady that had been nothing more than a whirlwind flying into the room as she had been at their first meeting. "Thank you for attending." She took a small step closer, darting a glance to her left before looking back at Hannah. "My uncle believes we met at my very first social occasion, which was Lady Stonehaven's ball."

She stepped back and Hannah gave her a tiny nod, a small smile fixed to her lips as she moved toward Lord

Greene, who had never met her before. She saw a footman murmur something to him, his eyes taking her in, a darkness in his expression that she did not think any sort of smile could hide.

"Miss Seymour," Lord Greene said loudly, clearly having heard her name from the footman. "You are acquainted with my niece, I believe."

Hannah curtsied again. "I am," she said, recalling what Miss Lewisham had said. "We were introduced at Lady Stonehaven's ball." She looked directly into Lord Greene's eyes, remembering with a sudden sinking of her stomach that Lord Greene did not ever allow his niece to go out of his sight. Would he be suspicious of her? Or had there been too many introductions for him to recall everyone directly? Lord Greene held her gaze for another moment, no smile on his face, assessing her before, finally, he bowed.

"You are very welcome," he said, gesturing for her to step a little more into the drawing room. She went at once, not saying anything more to him, knowing that Miss Hawkins was only a step behind her. Her breath ran from her as relief chased all through her, her shoulders relaxing as she looked around the room. The conversation and chatter were going on quite as normal, and the adjoining door was wide open also. More guests would be in there, she presumed, wondering if it could be the music room.

"Miss Seymour," Lady Ann was beside her in a

moment, her eyes bright as she looked up into Hannah's face. "I have heard from Lady Catherine that you are to attend the house party."

"Not only that," Miss Hawkins added, coming to join them and evidently overhearing the conversation, "but we are to make our way to the estate a little earlier, so that we might aid in final preparations."

"Which will give us all the more opportunity to find the ornament for Miss Lewisham," Lady Ann finished, looking quite delighted. "And if she is able to give it to her uncle before the betrothal is announced, then we will pray that she will find herself free of her engagement." A pointed look was given toward Hannah, who found herself blushing furiously, embarrassment climbing up into her eyes. She did not know what to say to this, quite certain that if Lord Bentham was freed of this engagement, then he certainly would not look in her direction again and that, even if he chose to do so, she would not allow herself to consider him. After all, he had allowed himself to show an interest in her whilst already knowing that he was betrothed.

"Let us hope so, for Miss Lewisham's sake," Miss Hawkins said with a gentle firmness to her voice. "She is deeply distraught." She glanced at the lady, only to look back at Hannah and then Lady Ann. "Although I cannot help but confess that I would very much like to know what the meaning of these ornaments is."

"And why they are so significant," Hannah

murmured, aware of the spark of interest that caught her heart, despite her own struggles. She *did* want to know what would drive a man to force his niece into marriage for the sake of a small ornament. Were they of great value or family significance? And if so, why did he appear so reluctant simply to ask for the ornament back, given that the betrothal could easily be brought to an end since the time for the marriage had passed? Was there really a clause in this supposed agreement?

"You are still a Shadow, Miss Seymour, even in your difficulties," Lady Ann murmured, her hand on Hannah's arm. "I heard what happened with your father. I am sorry he is so cruel to you."

Hannah looked up into her friend's face and felt her heart swell with gladness that she had such dear companions. "I am blessed to have you all with me," she said honestly. "I will not pretend that I am not confused by what has occurred, particularly as regards Lord Bentham, but I am now determined to go to this house party. I—"

A figure appeared just behind Miss Hawkins and Hannah stumbled to a stop, her eyes wide as she realized just who it was. Lord Bentham had strode into the room, his face a mask. There was no smile upon his handsome face, his jaw set and no spark in his dark blue eyes. Whilst the cut of his clothes and the style of his light brown hair spoke of time and effort being put into his appearance here this evening, there was something about his manner that suggested to Hannah that he was somewhat reluctant. There was a stiffness in his movements, a tight line of tension running straight through him. It seemed Lord Bentham did not want to be present here this evening.

He looked in her direction, snagging on her gaze, and Hannah instantly caught her breath, pulling her eyes in an entirely different direction, feeling heat climb up her neck and into her face.

"Might I presume that Lord Bentham has arrived?" Lady Ann asked softly, and Hannah nodded miserably. "Well, then, let us all stand together now, so that you will not have to speak to him alone." She smiled at Hannah as Miss Hawkins drew a little closer, keeping the small circle they had formed all the more intimate. Hannah let out her breath slowly, calming herself as best she could. Her heart was pounding, her chest tight, praying that he would not come closer and yet feeling his presence moving nearer to them all.

"I did not expect to see The Shadows here this evening."

Lord Bentham's voice made Hannah close her eyes tightly for a moment, trying to chase away her growing sense of tension, only to feel Lady Ann's hand on her arm. Opening her eyes, she let her friends speak for her.

"We are acquainted with Miss Lewisham, Lord Bentham," Lady Ann said in a nonchalant manner. "It was very kind of her to invite us."

Lord Bentham nodded but as Hannah dared to glance up at him, she saw no smile on his face or brightness in his eyes when speaking of his betrothed. She could not understand it, her heart aching as she looked away from him. Was this how he had felt when he had shown a distinct interest in her? Had he merely wanted her company and conversation rather than any true consideration? And now that the truth of his betrothal had come out, he was not even the least bit concerned as to how she herself might feel. He appeared to care nothing for the young lady and thus, Hannah concluded, he had never truly felt anything for her either.

"I am to speak to her uncle this evening," Lord Bentham replied, even though no one had asked him any such question. "There is a matter of grave importance and I—"

"Should you like to take a turn about the room, Miss Seymour?"

Hannah turned her head to see none other than Lady Haddington standing there beside her husband, her eyes darting angrily toward Lord Bentham for just a moment before returning to Hannah's face.

"I would, yes," Hannah said at once, hearing Lord Bentham begin to stammer but having no eagerness to hear what he was trying to say. "How good to see you here this evening, Lady Haddington."

Her friend smiled and begged the others to excuse

them, only for Hannah to feel a hand on her arm. Stunned, she stopped dead, turning slowly to see Lord Bentham stare back at her, his face draining of color as though he only just realized what he had done.

"My apologies, Miss Seymour," Lord Bentham said, holding up his hands. "I did not mean... I did intend to stop you, yes, but I..." Closing his eyes, he dropped his hands to his side. "I meant to ask if we might converse quietly at some point this evening and I did not want you to depart before I was able to ask you such a thing."

Hannah saw the color heighten in Lord Bentham's face and watched as his eyes darted this way and that, never quite resting on anything of note. She did not know what to say, wondering what it could be that he had to speak to her about and yet finding herself to be less than eager to hear it. She did not want to walk with him, did not want to hear him apologize or explain his betrothal, or whatever such a conversation would contain. She looked to her friends, who were all staring at Lord Bentham with the same astonishment and surprise in their expressions as she felt within her own heart.

"I do not think this evening is the most appropriate time, Lord Bentham," she told him calmly, aware of how he dropped his gaze and let out a long, exasperated breath. "Surely you can understand that tonight's soiree, with your betrothed present, is not at all the right time for us to speak."

He frowned. "She has told you, then, that we are supposedly to wed."

"Supposedly?" She felt her own cheeks warming but kept her voice steady, even though her hands curled into fists as she battled with the awkward tension rising within her. "You should be ashamed to be speaking of your betrothed in such a manner, Lord Bentham. Mayhap we will be able to do so for a few minutes at your house party." Making to turn away, Hannah heard Lord Bentham say something more, muttering under his breath. Turning her head, she looked back directly into his eyes, her brows knotting as she tried to work out what it was he had said. How could he speak of Miss Lewisham in such a manner? And why did he speak as though there was only the suggestion of their engagement rather than what she knew to be true? Lord Bentham lifted his eyes and held her gaze and she was astonished to see what appeared to be misery drifting into his expression.

"There is more to this than you might yet understand," Lord Bentham said, directing his words to everyone within the small group. "I have not spoken of it as yet, being uncertain as to whether or not I believed that this could be true, but now that I stand here, I..." He drifted off, looking utterly wretched and despite her own awkwardness, Hannah could not help but wonder what Lord Bentham spoke of. He was betrothed and soon to be wed. A house party was to take place to celebrate his engagement, but the expression on his face told her that he was deeply confused about something relating to his bride. Her heart began to soften toward him, only for her to turn her head away, refusing to allow her emotions to grasp a hold of her again.

"You are correct to state that now is not an appropriate time, however," Lord Bentham continued dully. "Mayhap at the house party itself, although if Miss Lewisham is speaking to you of our engagement then I cannot help but wonder if there is any real need for me to do so."

"What is it you wish to speak to us about?" Hannah heard herself asking, even though she did not look at Lord Bentham again. "If it is about your bride-to-be, then I can assure you that even though we are The Shadows, we will do nothing to try and bring her any shame or difficulty." Her eyes flicked up toward his and she saw nothing but despondency in his expression, her brows pulling together in confusion. "We will not try to find a way for you to end your betrothal due to some mistake or past misdemeanor on her part."

Lord Bentham let out a long breath and, lowering his head, ran one hand over his eyes.

"How little you must now think of me," he said, so softly that Hannah had to strain to hear him. "I have been a fool. It is little wonder that you now consider me so cruel. I—"

The sound of Lord Greene's voice filling the room,

calling his guests to the music room, broke through Lord Bentham's words. Everyone looked toward their host, only for Lord Bentham to step forward, reach out, and touch Hannah's hand. She jerked in surprise, stepping back and pulling her hand away from him, but Lord Bentham did not move or apologize. Instead, he looked into her face and she saw there an honest eagerness in his face, his eyes searching hers and his jaw working furiously, as if he were battling to keep his emotions under control.

"This is not as it seems," he told her, his voice low as the other guests began to move forward into the music room. "I must speak to The Shadows, for I will need your help in this matter. I do not wish to toss Miss Lewisham aside in any sort of cruel manner, I assure you, but still, there are questions that I must have help in answering. Can I rely on you to listen to me, at the very least?"

Hannah wanted to answer that this was a matter for all of The Shadows rather than just for herself, but something in Lord Bentham's eyes cried out that he wanted to explain it all to her, rather than to everyone. She fought the urge to throw a cruel response toward him, balling up her pain so that it might injure him as much as it could. Instead, she drew in a long breath, steadying herself and holding his gaze with as much strength as she could.

"I will listen to your explanation at an appropriate

time, Lord Bentham," she promised, despite her impulse to state that she would do no such thing. "But for the moment, let us go with Lord Greene into the music room."

She was astonished to see the immediate change in Lord Bentham's expression. Whilst his head dropped in relief, when he raised it, there was a faint anger in his eyes, his lips pulled taut as he turned his head to look in the direction of Lord Greene. Hannah felt her own curiosity growing, chasing away her own upset and confusion. What was it that troubled Lord Bentham so? She knew very well that Miss Lewisham was deeply upset and fearful of her uncle, so mayhap she had shared that with Lord Bentham. Perhaps he disliked Lord Greene on her behalf. No sooner had she thought of such a thing than Hannah pushed the idea away, knowing that Miss Lewisham would not have allowed herself to have such an intimacy with her betrothed when she was doing her utmost to escape from the engagement. She would not have said anything to Lord Bentham about her uncle, given that she had come to The Shadows for help. So there must be something more, something else, that now brought such a spark of anger into Lord Bentham's eyes.

"That is a relief, Miss Seymour."

Hannah caught movement beside her as the rest of The Shadows began to follow the guests into the music room, with Lady Haddington's hand resting on Hannah's shoulder for a moment, so as to encourage her into the room. She smiled tightly and nodded, feeling all manner of emotions clash together within her as she looked back into Lord Bentham's face.

"But of course, Lord Bentham," she said with a small inclination of her head. "I am part of The Shadows, as you know, and would be glad to hear whatever it is you wish to say in the hope that we might be able to assist you."

He pressed his lips together, the anger fading from his eyes. He watched her steadily for some moments, his eyes running over her face as though he was trying to commit her features to memory.

"I have been a fool, Miss Seymour," he told her, his voice soft and his words filled with frustration and pain. "It is only now that I see it. It has hit me with such force that I cannot even begin to consider what I have done." He shook his head, closed his eyes, and rubbed one hand down his face. "I thought to enjoy my own life for a little longer rather than consider anything of impor-tance, even though I knew that my heart was pulling me toward you. And now, I find myself betrothed and filled with regret that I did not turn away from my own arro-gance and selfishness, left with my own regrets haunting me like ghosts." Reaching out one hand, he waited until she gave him her own, her fingers trembling in his as she watched him bow over her hand, his lips only a breath away from her skin.

When he lifted his head and looked into her eyes, Hannah was struck by the sadness that was etched there. Without another word, he let go of her hand, inclined his head, and turned away, walking with long strides toward the music room. Hannah stared after him, a chill running all through her as she fought to understand all that had gone on. Surely Lord Bentham did not mean all that he had said? It could not be entirely true, for surely he had known that he was betrothed and would have to marry Miss Lewisham one day. Why, then, had he spoken of regret, of a desire to have drawn closer to her as though it might have saved him from his engagement?

"There is much still to say between you both, I think."

Hannah jerked in surprise, pulled from her thoughts by the gentle voice of Miss Hawkins.

"Do forgive me for startling you and for listening," Miss Hawkins said apologetically, "but I did not want to leave you alone with him."

"I thank you," Hannah answered, her voice still filled with surprise. "I confess, Miss Hawkins, I do not understand Lord Bentham at all. I feel so conflicted in my own sentiments and desires that I cannot even tell you what it is I wish from him at this present moment."

"That is quite understandable," Miss Hawkins replied, looping her arm through Hannah's and walking with her toward the music room, where Hannah knew

Lord Bentham would be. Would he be watching her as she entered? Or would he keep his face turned away, impassive and dark with his own emotions? "I think, for the present, we must just continue on as we are and thereafter, seek to speak to Lord Bentham as soon as is possible. It will, no doubt, be at his house party but it will give you both the time required to speak honestly." Her brows furrowed and she looked at Hannah. "Whatever he wishes to say, I believe he spoke the truth when he said to you that there was more to this than we knew."

"Perhaps I have judged him too harshly," Hannah murmured, only for Miss Hawkins to laugh and pat her arm.

"No, you have judged him quite fairly, Miss Seymour," she said with a firmness to her voice but with her eyes holding good humor. "You must not begin to judge your own actions for you have done nothing wrong. Lord Bentham *was* interested in your company —that was clear for us all to see—and if he now regrets pursuing his own interests and enjoyments rather than doing what he ought and following his heart, that is entirely his own fault." Her voice dropped as they entered the room. "You are quite within your rights to feel grievously injured in that alone, Miss Seymour."

Hannah let out a long, slow breath and nodded, unable to help herself as she glanced about the room, knowing that Lord Bentham was somewhere within. It was a very odd sensation to find herself now seeking out the very gentleman who had caused her so much difficulty, but there was something within her now that could not be held back. With only a few words, he had reignited a spark within her and it was not one that could easily be put out.

Her breath hitched as she caught his gaze, seeing how his blue eyes were fixed to her, his elbow resting on the arm of the chair he sat on, his head low. There was such a deep intensity there, as though he were longing after something he could not have and Hannah felt it run right through her, like a chill that comes on the first day of winter. It lingered on her skin, making her breathless as Miss Hawkins urged her into a seat. Turning her head away, Hannah closed her eyes and took in a few steadying breaths, trying to make sense of all that she felt, trying to sort out each emotion one by one. But all she could feel was Lord Bentham's eyes still lingering on her, heat burning her skin as she kept her gaze fixed on the pianoforte at the front of the room. A sense of trepidation built as she considered the house party that she would soon be attending, wondering just what would be said and what Lord Bentham would share with her. Would it change anything? Would he ask her to help bring an end to his engagement so that he might pursue her in Miss Lewisham's place? Hannah closed her eyes tightly, her hands balling into fists. She could not help him, if that was what he asked. She was a

Shadow, and thus knew that her first duty was to help Miss Lewisham, even if everything within her wanted to be close to Lord Bentham.

Even if that meant turning her back on what could be a happy future and instead accepting the fate that would be waiting for her in its place.

5
____

The papers sat neatly on George's desk, but he did not want to look at them. Ever since Lord Greene had presented them to him, George had found himself recoiling, refusing even to touch them for fear that the words contained within would stick to his skin.

The agreement was there, however, no matter how hard he pulled himself away from it. His own solicitors had found nothing of the sort and yet the papers Lord Greene had in his possession appeared to be quite legitimate. His father's signature was present, as was Lord Greene's. However, one side held Lord Greene's seal, but his own father's seal was notable by its absence. George gritted his teeth and picked up the scroll of papers, setting them to one side and praying silently that he would find another way to remove himself from this betrothal before the house party had even begun.

Sighing, George picked up his glass of whisky and took a sip, dropping into a chair by the glowing fire. Thus far, the month of August had been glorious in all its sunshine and warmth, but this side of George's estate was always rather cold no matter the temperature outside and thus, he had always insisted that a fire be laid in the grate. With another sigh, he looked into the embers, wondering if the best thing to do would be to burn the papers Lord Greene had brought him. After all, if he did that, then there would be no evidence that his father had ever made any such arrangement. He toyed with the idea for a few minutes, even though he knew such a thing was quite foolish. He could not do that, not when it would be both wrong and inconsequential. Lord Greene knew that the papers were legitimate and, given what The Shadows knew of his betrothal, it seemed that Miss Lewisham was having no particular difficulty in speaking of it to anyone she wished. Grimacing, George threw back the rest of his whisky. Miss Lewisham was not plain, with her dark hair and blue eyes, but there was something reserved in her manner whenever she even glanced at him. They had been formally introduced by her uncle, of course, but he had found her quiet and listless, her eyes rather dull whenever she deigned to look at him. He did not think he had even seen her smile.

Aware of how his heart squeezed with the pain that came with such recollections, how his sense of regrets piled one atop the other deep within him, George rose and poured himself more whisky. It was all much too late. He could not think of Miss Seymour now, not when he was entirely unsure as to whether or not he would have to marry Miss Lewisham. If he had pursued Miss Seymour, if he had allowed the feelings in his heart to grow, then he might now be in a very different situation indeed. Of course, he could merely state that the time stated in the agreement had passed and thus detract himself from the betrothal, but his sense of gentlemanly conduct would not permit him to do so. Miss Lewisham had not been to London except on one previous occasion, for the very start of her Season. Her father had become unwell and so they had returned to the estate, where some time later, the late Lord Greene had passed from life to death, leaving his brother to inherit the title, given that he had no sons of his own. It was not at all the done thing to throw aside such an agreement because of grief and mourning, for he was expected to be understanding and considerate of the circumstances such as they were, and yet there was still a great reluctance within him. Groaning aloud, he pushed his head into his hands, his glass of whisky now on the table beside him.

A scratch at the door caught his attention and he

lifted his head, leaning it back in the chair before calling for the butler to enter.

"Your guests seek an audience with you, Lord Bentham."

Immediately, George sat bolt upright in his chair, staring at the door as he gestured for his butler to allow them entry. He did not know who would arrive, praying that it might be Miss Seymour rather than any of the other ladies—although quite what he would say, he had not yet considered.

"Lord Haddington." George's stomach dropped but he rose quickly, not wanting his friend to consider him rude nor willing to allow Lord Haddington to see the regret that swelled in George's chest. "Good afternoon. I trust you have settled in?"

Lord Haddington nodded, folding himself into a chair before George could invite him to sit down. "I have," he said, looking at George with a somewhat stern expression, his brows low over his eyes and his mouth pulled tight. "Miss Lewisham and her uncle are due to arrive tomorrow, I understand."

"In two days hence," George corrected, no eagerness to see his betrothed quickening his heart but rather feeling such a sense of dread that he shuddered violently. "As are Lord Kerr, Baron and Baroness Hollander, and Miss Vonage with her parents, Viscount and Viscountess Florence."

Lord Haddington nodded slowly, watching George

with such a firm eye that George felt himself grow rather uncomfortable. He shifted in his seat, then got up, ready to offer his friend a drink when Lord Haddington spoke again.

"You do not wish to marry Miss Lewisham, I think."

George's stomach dropped but he turned to his friend, spreading his hands. "I will not pretend that I am enamored with her, no."

"Then," Lord Haddington continued with a frown, "might I ask why you proposed to the lady if you have no real interest in her? I cannot say that I have been pleased with how you have conducted yourself, old boy, particularly when it comes to Miss Seymour."

George swallowed hard and dropped his gaze, trying to think of what to say. Thus far, he had not spoken of the truth of his engagement, although had Miss Seymour been willing to listen to him at the soiree some ten days ago, he would have been willing to tell her the truth of it then and, mayhap, to beg for her help. It had all been so very confusing and difficult, which was why, he considered, he had not spoken of it to anyone as yet. Even to Lord Paxton, who had become a very close friend, he had not found it possible to say a single word.

"There is a good deal more to this situation than first meets the eye," he said as Lord Haddington frowned. "Forgive me for my awkwardness, Lord Haddington, but I have been so very confused of late that I have found it difficult to make even the smallest of speeches without losing my train of thought." He shook his head and threw one hand out toward the door. "And then this house party was thrust in my lap without any real agreement from myself, which I simply *cannot* understand, and now I am in a situation where I am so tightly bound to my current course that I fear that I shall have to wed Miss Lewisham even though I have no real wish to."

Lord Haddington blinked slowly, his eyes cat-like as he watched George, taking in everything he was saying and considering it with evidently infinite care.

"You mean to say that you did not propose to Miss Lewisham?" he asked, sounding rather confused. "And yet you find yourself engaged to her?"

George closed his eyes and let out a long, heavy sigh. "That is it precisely," he said with a shake of his head. "I know that there is very little sense in such a statement, but I think I shall keep my explanations for the present, until I am able to speak to everyone." Everyone, of course, meant specifically Miss Seymour, for George was all the more aware of his eager desire to explain to her what had happened, even though that would not extract him from his current predicament. "I had hoped, in a small way, that mayhap The Shadows would be able to help me in all of this."

Lord Haddington harrumphed, shifting slightly in his chair. "I am sure they will be very glad to," he said with a lift of his shoulders. "In fact, why do you not come to speak to them this afternoon? They will be ready to join you in the drawing room very soon, I am sure."

George nodded slowly, his lip caught between his teeth as he considered. "It would be wise," he said, feeling a twisting in his gut as he thought of having to tell them everything that had happened, ashamed that his feelings toward Miss Seymour had only burst to life in the moments since he had found himself bound to another. To look into her face and to try to explain what had occurred would be torturous indeed.

"Do you think you will have your thoughts in coherent order within the hour?" Lord Haddington asked, his eyes flickering with curiosity but his tone one of kindness. "I can see from the look on your face that you are in something of a bind and I apologize for being a little harsh."

George shook his head, holding up one hand. "You do not need to apologize," he told his friend firmly. "You are quite correct in what you stated. I *did* show an interest in Miss Seymour, and I confess that I was certainly eager to consider taking matters forward with her."

"Then why did you not?"

Closing his eyes again, George tipped his head back and blew out a long breath, feeling shame climb up his spine, sending a flurry of heat into his face. "Because I allowed myself to be swayed by another," he said, thinking of Lord Kerr, whom he had invited to the house party also. Opening his eyes, he saw Lord Haddington frown. "Not that such a thing is any sort of an excuse," he said quickly, "for I am fully aware it was entirely my own selfish nature that encouraged me to set aside the regard that was building for Miss Seymour." He passed a hand over his eyes, still filled with a sense of shame. "I thought I could enjoy my life as I pleased for some time yet, and convinced myself that my feelings were not of any great significance and that there was no need for me to find a suitable bride despite the feelings within my heart."

"So you chose to set your feelings aside in place of your own selfishness," Lord Haddington said bluntly. "You would not be the first gentleman to do so."

George shook his head, not wanting to even attempt to make himself feel better in any way. He might not be the first gentleman to behave in such a manner, but that did not detract from his spiraling sense of remorse.

"It feels as though I have pushed Miss Seymour all the further away," George finished with a heavy heart. "I will tell you of this also, even though it only adds to my shame, but I was speaking of this desire to live as I pleased, to push away my inclination toward Miss Seymour, and was, in fact, proudly boasting about my decision, such as it was." He winced, feeling as though he were confessing his sins aloud but knowing it was best for him to share all that he had done thus far. "When I turned my head, I saw that Miss Seymour was present, having overheard a good deal of what I had said."

Lord Haddington lifted one eyebrow, but said nothing, keeping his own counsel for the present.

"I cannot imagine what she must be feeling, having heard me declare such a thing only now to be engaged to Miss Lewisham," George finished, his gut twisting. "Mayhap, within my own heart, that is what has kept me from speaking to her—and to you all—about what has happened."

Lord Haddington let out a long breath, his brow still lifted as he looked at George. George had no choice but to wait for judgment to fall, his breath rattling out of him, his fingers tense as they clutched the arms of his chair.

"I do not pretend to know Miss Seymour well," Lord Haddington said quietly, his words slow and chosen carefully, "but she is a gentle soul who has endured nothing but indifference and displeasure from her own father. From what I know, she is in a difficult bind herself at present..." Trailing off, Lord Haddington frowned suddenly, stopping himself. "But I will not say more on that, for it is her right to tell whoever she chooses about such things."

George frowned also, a concern for Miss Seymour rising in his mind, for she had never said anything about a difficult situation with her father, but perhaps she had felt no need to do so, considering that they had not enjoyed a particularly long acquaintance. What was it that troubled her now and was he the cause of it? Mayhap her father had thought him eagerly interested in his daughter and, as such, had been hoping for a courtship. With his swift departure from London, had Miss Seymour's father decided that his absence had been his daughter's fault?

"My reason for saying such things is so that you are aware her heart has already been injured a good deal and thereafter to beg you not to do any more to harm her."

Guilt swarmed over George like a thousand buzzing bees. He dropped his head into his hands, aware that he had already injured Miss Seymour a good deal. "I will take great care," he promised, his eyes fixed to the floor. "What a great fool I have been."

Walking toward the drawing room, with Lord Haddington having already gone ahead in order to give George a little more time to think on what he was to say, George took slow steps, his brow furrowed and his eyes downcast. What Lord Haddington had said about Miss Seymour had brought him a good deal of strife, realizing just how little he knew of her circumstances and feeling a surge of protectiveness toward her. It shamed him to think of just how easily he had managed to push such feelings aside, how selfish and arrogant he had been in deciding to pursue his own pleasures rather than what might have been with Miss Seymour.

"Oh, excuse me."

George stumbled back as the object of his thoughts suddenly opened a door to his left, with the door itself almost catching his arm. For a moment, Miss Seymour's mouth opened and closed with no sound coming from her, only for him to see a small flash of amusement in her eyes.

"I do apologize, Miss Seymour," he said with a quick bow. "Are you on your way to the drawing room?"

She nodded, her cheeks now a little pink. "I am," she told him, dropping her head, "but I appear to have become a little lost."

He watched her for a long moment, his heart stirring within him as he remembered how close a friendship they had begun to build between them only a few weeks before.

"I—I would be glad to show you," he stammered, a little awkwardly. "It is just along here and I..." Closing his eyes for a moment, he winced. "Miss Seymour, there is a tension between us which I am certain that you yourself feel."

"That is quite true," came the gentle voice of Miss Seymour. "You are clearly not unaware of it yourself."

Opening his eyes, George let out his breath quickly and began to speak, not wanting to miss the opportunity to tell her what was now on his mind now that he had spoken to Lord Haddington.

"I cannot imagine what you must think of me," he said, the words coming out of him in a rush. "First to overhear my arrogance and pride in stating that I had decided to do nothing but enjoy myself this Season, and then to hear that I am, in fact, betrothed…" His words came to a stop and he looked wretchedly at Miss Seymour, his heart burning with pain as he saw the way her eyes filled with tears. "I have hurt you enormously, Miss Seymour, I know, and for you to come to my estate, willing to assist in the preparations for the house party, is more than I deserve."

She swallowed and looked away, but he still heard her shaky intake of breath. He wanted to cry out to her again but instead said nothing, keeping his mouth closed so that she would not think he was making excuses for what had been a great deal of wrongdoing.

"I am not here solely for your benefit, Lord Bentham," she said without looking at him. "Do not be under any illusion."

"I am not," he said hoarsely, more than aware that The Shadows would have convinced her to attend. "This must be very difficult for you."

Her gray eyes clouded, and she looked up at him, tilting her head just a fraction. Her brows lowered, a line forming between her eyes as she studied him. George did not know what to say or what to do, beads of sweat forming on his brow.

"Why did you say such things?"

Her question astonished him and it took George a few minutes to realize what she was waiting for. When he finally opened his mouth to speak, he saw Miss Seymour fold her arms, as if protecting herself from whatever it was that would come from him.

"I have nothing to give you but the truth," he said softly, lowering his eyes. "It was a decision I made solely for what I believed was my own benefit. I did not want to think about securing a wife, with one of my friends convincing me that I did not need to dwell on any feelings or the like at present." Again, he lifted his shoulders, spreading his hands wide. "And like a fool, Miss Seymour, I believed him and chose to do what *I* wanted without consideration for my feelings and those of your own."

Miss Seymour hesitated for a moment, then let out a long breath. "I see," she said, rather dully. "And yet now you are betrothed?"

"That is precisely what I wished to explain to you," he said at once, relieved that she had brought the matter up. "I am not betrothed because I wish to be but rather because I have no other choice but to be so." He saw her brow flicker with a frown although she said nothing. "I would tell it to you now, if you so wish?"

Miss Seymour hesitated again and she looked away.

"Are you to speak of this to The Shadows?" she asked softly, clearly worried that such a thing might be inappropriate for her to hear on her own. "I should not like to be the only one with additional knowledge at what is already a rather difficult time."

He nodded and swallowed hard, trying to explain. "I will tell everyone," he said with a shrug, "if I have to. But I should like to explain to you first, Miss Seymour."

Again, she looked at him for a few moments before giving him the tiniest of nods, her eyes still darting from here to there and never quite managing to linger on his face. George, his stomach swirling with a sudden anxiety, cleared his throat gruffly and began to speak.

"First of all, I will say that I regret all that you overheard," he began, seeing the immediate slight narrowing of Miss Seymour's eyes. "Not that I am merely sorry that you overheard it, but I truly am sorry for even stating it." He rubbed at his forehead with his knuckles, trying to find the right words to tell her the truth without making himself sound righteous and arrogant. "I have realized, with what has occurred, that I was nothing more than selfish. I convinced myself that I did not want to think of a steady future with a wife and an heir and that I could push aside such feelings in order to revel in the enjoyment of the Season." He swallowed hard, aware of the sensation of his heart being slowly exposed to Miss Seymour, the painful ripping of all that he had kept hidden away. "How foolish I have been, Miss Seymour."

Again, Miss Seymour said nothing. Her gaze remained narrowed, her eyes sparkling with silver and dancing with both curiosity and uncertainty. Her arms were folded over her chest, protecting herself from him, considering him still to be some sort of enemy.

"Lord Greene—the uncle to Miss Lewisham—appeared at my door one afternoon, when I was expecting Lord Kerr," George continued, somewhat hoarsely. "He told me that there is an agreement between our families, made by Miss Lewisham's late father and my own. I did not know anything of it, but the papers were duly produced and it appears that he is quite correct." He swallowed. "The only thing that is lacking is my father's seal, which the current Lord Greene states he is certain I will find on my own papers, once I discover them."

Miss Seymour took in a sharp intake of breath at this, her eyes widening and her hands falling to her sides. There was no color in her cheeks now, nothing but sheer astonishment at what he had told her.

"If I discover the papers and they bear no seal, then I have every right to state that I cannot be held to the agreement. But if it is present with a signature and seal, then... then I am obliged to do as is required," he confirmed, a heavy weight sitting on his shoulders.

"And could not Lord Greene merely have added his

late brother's seal at a later date?" Miss Seymour asked, her voice unsteady. "Could it be falsified?"

He shook his head, wishing it could be so. "The seal is clearly old," he said regretfully. "If it were new, it would be very easy to see." Letting out another long breath, he gestured hopelessly. "Miss Lewisham was expected to wed me within a few months of her mourning period coming to an end."

Miss Seymour blinked rapidly, one hand now pressed against her chest. Her eyes were wide and she was staring at him in disbelief.

"As the betrothal arrangement was not known by her uncle until this moment, a good time after her mourning period has ended, I am still expected to continue on as has been arranged."

"But how can this be?" Miss Seymour asked, reaching out and, much to his surprise, one hand grasping his arm. "How can you not have known anything about your own engagement?"

She was standing closer to him now, and rather than quietening his anxious heart, her nearness served only to draw it to a galloping pace. For a moment, he forgot what it was she had asked of him, only to see her frown return and thus forced himself to gather his thoughts.

"I knew nothing of it because my father never spoke of it to me," he said as honestly as he could. "Nor my mother. My father was, as you might recall, taken from this earth rather swiftly, with no suggestion of illness and the like." His chest felt heavy as his mind brought back the memory of how his father had died clutching at his chest, gasping about the pain in his heart. "Lord Greene has stated that there is a copy of these papers here, that my father had them also. I have every intention of finding these papers, for I must know for certain whether or not this is the truth of what my father desired for me."

After such a long speech, George felt quite worn out. Miss Seymour still had her hand on his arm, still looked up at him in astonishment, but he could find no words to say that would add anything to what he had already explained. Instead, he simply looked into her eyes, almost able to sense how her mind was working through all that he had said, in an attempt to straighten it out completely and fully understand it.

"Goodness."

Miss Seymour let out a long breath, her hand loosening on his arm and her head dropping just a little, so that her eyes were fixed on something just over his right shoulder. George lifted his hand and placed it on hers, wanting to give a little comfort as well as take some from her in return.

"It is rather overwhelming, I confess," he said, a little darkly. "But what else can I do but find these papers? My father clearly had a reason for his choice, and I must—"

"But this is extraordinary," Miss Seymour interrupted, her eyes suddenly ablaze with excitement—an excitement he could not even *begin* to understand—and her hand tightening under his. "Goodness, Lord Bentham, this changes everything. We must speak to the others at once!"

She made to turn and tug him along the hallway, but George refused to be moved. Standing steadfastly, he waited until she turned back toward him, his brow lowering as he watched her, unable to fathom the reason for her exuberance in the face of this otherwise desperate situation.

"I do not understand, Miss Seymour," he told her, his breath coming quickly as she came back toward him, her eyes still bright and a small smile catching the corners of her mouth. "I have told you everything and confessed to you that I am engaged to a lady I know nothing about and have no wish to know, and you react with delight?" A small stab of hurt pierced his heart, even though he knew he had no right to feel any such thing. "Surely you cannot be glad that this situation is upon me, even though I have behaved cruelly toward you."

Miss Seymour searched his face, her smile fading and the light disappearing from her eyes. "I should hope that you know me better than that, Lord Bentham," she said with a ring of reproof in her words. "I have never delighted in anyone's situation when it is as difficult as this." Her lips twisted and lines marred her brow. "Do you truly think that I would be so cruel?"

George let out his breath in a whoosh, aware that, yet again, he had brought pain to Miss Seymour without intention. "You are quite right, Miss Seymour," he said, suddenly realizing that he was still holding her hand, that her fingers were tight in his own. Heat began to spiral up his arm as he glanced down at their joined hands, wondering if this meant as much to her as it did to him at this present moment. "I do know you to be a kind and gentle soul, who has not even a trace of cruelty within her." He bowed over her hand as he had done so before, only to drop a kiss to her skin, unable to prevent himself from doing so. The touch of his lips on her skin made her start, but much to his relief, she did not let go.

"This must be greatly confusing to you, Lord Bentham, but I assure you that if you come with me and tell The Shadows all that you have told me, then this matter can be much more easily resolved than you might think. Unless..." The lines in her forehead deepened as she frowned, her hand pulling slowly from his. "Unless, of course, you *do*, in fact, wish to marry her?"

George's reaction was immediate. "No, no!" he exclaimed, throwing up his hands. "No, indeed, I have no intention of continuing with this marriage, such as it is. I do not want to marry Miss Lewisham." Reaching out one hand toward her, he tried to fill his voice with as much conviction as he could. "I swear to you, Miss Seymour, I want none other than you, even though I believe it would now be quite impossible."

These sweet words did not appear to have much of an impact on Miss Seymour for she did not put out her hand to him, her mouth in a firm line. She was not ready to hear anything such as that from him, he realized, not yet when there had already been too much said. The urge to tell her that he realized just how much of a mistake he had made had been deep within himself, but it had been spoken too early, making him feel rather foolish.

"Might I suggest that we go at once to where the others are, Lord Bentham," Miss Seymour said with a firmness that took him aback. "They will need to hear it from you at once. As you said yourself, there is more to this situation than there first appears. Only this time, it is you who does not know it."

George, rather nonplussed, gave a jerk of his head and began to stride down the hallway, leaving her to follow behind. The moment they had shared where she had taken his hand and looked into his eyes was gone, already fading away like an early morning mist. Whatever it was that Miss Seymour wanted to share with The Shadows, whatever difference it would make, he would do as she asked without question. Perhaps later there would come an opportunity for them both to talk a little more, although what good it would do, he could not say. George felt his spirits sink a little lower as he continued along the hallway, realizing that no matter what he felt, he would have to marry Miss Lewisham unless something happened that could allow him to cry off without any smudging of her reputation. It had been ridiculous for him to make such a declaration to Miss Seymour without thinking of the situation he was currently in.

Shaking his head, George pushed open the drawing room door, holding it open for Miss Seymour to walk through. The rest of The Shadows were already there, alongside Lord Haddington and Lord Paxton. They looked up at them both as one, the conversation fading away almost immediately with a look of surprise quickly forming on Lady Haddington's face at the sight of Miss Seymour emerging behind him.

"I can hardly believe this," Miss Seymour said at once, not even attempting to explain what had happened between herself and George only a few moments before, "but it seems as though Lord Bentham has also had no knowledge or awareness of his proposal." Her arms flung out wide as the other ladies looked from one to the other. "The betrothal was agreed upon by his late father and Miss Lewisham's late father, but only Lord Greene has a legitimate copy." Her eyes darted toward him, a smile on her face that he could not understand. "Lord Bentham is searching for these papers so that he might know for certain whether or not he is obliged to continue with the betrothal. But he certainly does not *wish* to marry the lady, just as she does not wish to marry him."

George blinked in astonishment, looking for the

surprise on the other faces but finding very little there. Evidently, they were all well aware that Miss Lewisham did not want to marry him, even though he was sure they were not particularly well acquainted.

"Then we must speak to Miss Lewisham the moment she arrives!" Lady Haddington exclaimed, her eyes wide and a broad smile on her lips, her hand reaching out to grasp her husband's hand tightly. "Goodness, she will be very relieved indeed."

"And if we can work together, then mayhap we will be able to free her from this engagement," Lady Catherine said, just as George saw Lady Ann nudge her arm. Lady Catherine flushed crimson but did not look away, holding George's gaze with a sharpness in her eye that made him want to drop his head. Evidently, she was all too aware of what he had done to hurt Miss Seymour and was upset with him for doing so.

"Wait!" Miss Seymour exclaimed, the brightness in her eyes fading as she sank down into a chair, her elbows on her lap, her hands now propping up her chin. "If we free her from her engagement, then her uncle might..." She did not say anything more and whilst George did not fully understand, he quickly realized that something was very wrong when it came to Miss Lewisham and her uncle.

"Lord Greene is not a good man?" he queried, moving to the side of the room to pour himself a rather large brandy, hoping it would give him a little more strength than he had at present, for with all that had been said, all that had been declared, he found himself quite weary. "What is it Miss Lewisham fears?"

He turned to see Miss Seymour exchange a glance with Miss Hawkins, who gave an almost imperceptible nod. Then, Miss Seymour cleared her throat and gave him a tight smile.

"Miss Lewisham has been instructed to find something within this house," she began, making George frown. "Something that was given by her late father to yours, at the time of the betrothal agreement."

"Then why does she not merely ask for it?"

"She does not know why her uncle refuses to permit her to do such a thing," Miss Seymour continued with a shrug. "But that is why Lord Greene is insisting that the marriage go ahead. Evidently, since you are a gentleman, he expects you to keep the betrothal agreement even though the time stated in the papers has passed."

George grimaced. "I would do so, of course. If she was in her mourning period when the time came for our wedding, even though I was unaware of it, I could not hold such a thing against her."

"Indeed," Miss Seymour murmured.

George opened his mouth to ask her what this object was, but Miss Seymour waved one hand and continued to speak.

"Miss Lewisham's mother still lives, the widowed Lady Greene," Miss Seymour added, as George took a sip of his brandy, a little surprised to hear this. He had not heard Miss Lewisham or Lord Greene mention her. "However, Lord Greene has had her placed in the Dower house and will not allow her daughter to see her nor allow Lady Greene to depart the house to come to London."

George frowned hard, his gut twisting with both sympathy and anger that a gentleman could behave so cruelly toward his own family. "And what are his reasons for doing so?" he asked, his brows knotting as he glanced around the room. "What possesses him to think that such behavior is appropriate?"

Lady Ann sat forward. "It is to ensure that Miss Lewisham finds this ornament, whether she is only engaged or wed to you," she said quietly. "An incentive, of the most cruel sort."

The bottom seemed to drop out of George's stomach as he stared at Lady Ann, wanting to hear her say that it was not as bad as what he had just heard, but that strained, angry expression remained on not only her features but also on the rest of those in the room.

"I should confess to you now that I did attempt to force your hand when it came to this house party," Lord Paxton interrupted, clearing his throat gruffly. "We were all quite astonished to hear of your betrothal and certainly, Miss Lewisham did not want you to know any of her own predicament for fear you might react poorly and bring down her uncle's ire upon her head. We thought you wanted this engagement, that you wanted to marry the lady, and thus we had to find a way to help Miss Lewisham and ensure that either her marriage to you would bring the secure return of her mother, or that if the betrothal was to come to an end, we would find a way to ensure that Lady Greene was released from the Dower house in some way."

"But now that we know you are as astonished as Miss Lewisham about this engagement and that you, too, wish to find a way to bring it to an end, we can tell you everything," Miss Hawkins said with a note of relief in her voice. "And we can all work together to not only help Miss Lewisham and her mother, but to help you find these supposed papers. The ornament might very well be with them also."

"So it seems," George murmured, still finding it all quite overwhelming and deciding that the best thing to do for the present was to sit down and allow his thoughts to settle. He did just that, nursing his glass of brandy and running one hand over his eyes.

"I do not think now that this house party is a particularly good idea," he muttered as Lord Paxton let out a wry chuckle. "But I see now that it must be done. Lord Greene does not allow Miss Lewisham to even step out of his sight for a moment and certainly would not allow her to attend here alone."

Miss Seymour nodded sagely. "She is bringing this ornament with her," she told him. "The gentleman figure, from what I recall. It will give us an idea of what the lady figurine might look like."

Lord Haddington frowned hard. "And her uncle will simply allow that?"

Lady Ann shrugged. "I believe Lord Greene attempts to rule over his niece by fear," she said, as Miss Seymour dropped her gaze, her cheeks coloring just a little. "He will not expect her to do anything other than what he has asked."

There was silence for a moment or two and then George saw Miss Seymour lift her head. Her eyes were flint, her shoulders set, and her back now ramrod straight.

"Then he will discover that there is more strength to her than he ever imagined," she said, her voice low and yet filling the room. "And that, I am sure, will be his downfall."

6

———

The next few days were a flurry of activity. The day had arrived for the guests to appear and whilst the house was ready, The Shadows certainly were not. They had searched high and low for these papers and the ornament, with Lord Paxton, Miss Hawkins, and Lady Catherine even venturing to the dusty attic to search for them. When they had reappeared, somewhat dustier than they were before, Hannah had felt her heart soar with hope, only for their sad shakes of the head to bring her hopes to the depths once more.

Lord Bentham had said very little. Ever since they had spoken at length, he had been quiet and reserved. At times, she caught him staring into space, his eyes seeming to look at something that was not quite there. Clearly, it was a great astonishment for him to know that there was more to Miss Lewisham's story than he had ever expected, and even more of a shock to know that she was in such a desperate situation. She wondered what it was he thought, and often lingered on the tender words that he had expressed when they had met in the hallway. It had not been at all the correct situation for him to express such sentiments, but nevertheless, his words still lingered, swooping around her heart and begging to be allowed in to heal her wounds.

"You are thinking on him again."

Hannah blushed furiously as Miss Hawkins came to sit down beside her, glancing in the direction of Lord Bentham, who was sitting across the room, a book on his knee but his eyes nowhere near it.

"You should speak to him," Miss Hawkins said encouragingly. "How shall you ever cross this great divide that has grown between you unless you speak openly?"

Hannah shook her head. "I cannot trust him," she said in a low voice. "Not yet, at least. He may have spoken beautiful words, but I cannot tell whether or not they came from the place of his heart. What if he was just overwhelmed with all that has occurred and spoke without consideration?"

"And there is a good deal you have to forgive him for also," Miss Hawkins interrupted, touching Hannah's arm. "Even if you do believe what he has said, he *did* make the decision to turn away from you in search of his own pleasures."

Hannah nodded, knowing that such a pain would not easily leave her. It was one thing to trust what he said but quite another to let go of what he had chosen to do. That would mean beginning anew, believing that nothing like that would happen again, that the words he said would not be thrown asunder for the sake of his own self-interest.

Glancing up, she saw Lord Bentham looking directly at her and immediately dropped her gaze, flushing a little as Miss Hawkins smiled understandingly, her gaze gentle.

"And we have not yet found the papers or the ornament," Hannah murmured, deciding to move the subject from one thing to the next. "Lord Bentham does look quite distraught."

Miss Hawkins sighed and slumped in her chair in a most unladylike fashion—not that Hannah herself thought anything of it. "There must be somewhere we have not yet searched," she mused, a frown creasing her forehead. "This estate is very large indeed and whilst I know he has the staff searching also, there surely is some small place that has been forgotten."

Hannah nodded, her lips twisting as she considered what they ought to do next. Lord Bentham had slowly sunk into despondency as the time drew near for his guests to arrive. Once they came, he would have to play the part of host, unable to simply set his attention onto anything else other than them.

She frowned, looking back at Lord Bentham and feeling a surge of sympathy that she did not, in fact, want to let penetrate her heart. Despite that, she remembered what she had said when there had been mention of Lord Greene and his cruelty toward Miss Lewisham. How much had that situation resonated with her own? She had felt an anger begin to settle over her, angry that Lord Greene would treat his niece and his sister-in-law with such ruthlessness, and then, within that, had come an anger for her own circumstances. That had not faded away but rather had grown slowly, settling within her. Why should she continue to buckle under her father's cruel ways, just as so many others did? He did not love her or treat her with any kindness, and all she had done thus far was give in to her fear of him. She had struggled to find any sort of courage and even the thought of doing as Lady Haddington had offered and going to the Haddington estate rather than returning home after the house party had filled her with dread. But why would she return when she knew what her father was planning for her? Yes, her reputation would be damaged if she stayed far from her father's house, but was she bold enough to risk it?

In a sudden motion, Hannah rose to her feet, startling Miss Hawkins, and strode across the room toward Lord Bentham. He stared at her in surprise, then rose to his feet in evident astonishment, inclining his head as though they were greeting each other for the first time that day.

"Lord Bentham," she said with a good deal of firmness, "your guests are due to arrive within a few hours. Instead of merely sitting here moping, might we not make a better use of our time?"

Lord Bentham cleared his throat, looking rather surprised. "What do you suggest, Miss Seymour?" he asked, clearly taken aback. "To be truthful, I would be grateful for any suggestions you might have."

She smiled at him, still feeling a good deal of tension within her but refusing to give it any sort of consideration. "I know that you say that we have searched everywhere, and the staff have all been fully involved, but surely there must be *somewhere* that we are yet to look."

Lord Bentham's face fell and he shook his head. "I am not convinced," he stated with resignation. "I am beginning to believe that my father never received such papers. And as for the ornament..." Shrugging, he looked away for a moment, his lips thin.

"And your mother has responded to your letter?"

He sighed and nodded. "She states that she recalls my father discussing it but does not know of any papers." A small, wry smile caught the corner of his mouth, his eyes alight for just a moment. "She was not the sort of mother who cared much about her children."

Hannah drew in a long breath and then exhaled

slowly, trying to consider what they should do next. She did not want to just give up, quite convinced in her own mind that these papers had to be somewhere. If they had no seal upon them, then there was an easy way for Lord Bentham to extract himself, and if they could find the ornament Lord Greene requested, then there was a chance for Miss Lewisham to find the freedom she so desperately desired.

Lord Greene might be all the more amiable if Miss Lewisham was able to give him what he sought, but Hannah knew that The Shadows would do whatever they could to help both Miss Lewisham and her mother, regardless of whether it was found or not.

"Might I suggest, Lord Bentham, that we go from room to room, looking in every nook, in every single space, until we are quite certain that the papers and the ornament are not within this house anywhere?"

"Miss Seymour," Lord Bentham said, shuffling his feet, his gaze darting from here to there in a somewhat awkward fashion. "That is a wise suggestion indeed, but I must confess that I think it will take such a great deal of time that I—"

"We can begin before your guests arrive and, once they appear, we will take whatever opportunity we can to continue," she said, interrupting him and seeing the astonishment on his face that she had done so with such evident determination. "Come now, Lord Bentham. Either you wish to find these papers or you do not. Only when we have searched everywhere thoroughly will we know for certain whether or not they are within."

"I could not agree more, Miss Seymour," Miss Hawkins said, coming to join them, her eyes seeming to glow with either mirth, pride, or a mixture of both. "A capital idea. I should like to help, of course, and I am sure that the other Shadows will wish to do so also."

Hannah smiled at her friend but then turned her gaze back to Lord Bentham, looking at him for a long moment, until, finally, he sighed and then nodded.

"Very well, Miss Seymour. I will admit that your strategy makes sense. My guests will be here within a few hours, but I think everything is quite prepared."

"I am sure it is," she said, knowing that the staff here were thoroughly prepared for all that would soon be required of them. "Then might we begin?"

Miss Hawkins held up one delicate finger. "I shall remain here and ensure that the others know what your intentions are," she said, an entirely innocent expression on her face. Hannah felt a flare of heat crawl up into her chest, fully aware of what her friend was attempting to do and not quite certain whether or not she was glad of it.

"There is no need for that, Miss Hawkins," Lord Bentham replied, sounding a little surprised. "I am sure that I—"

"I insist," Miss Hawkins replied, interrupting him. "I will not detain you any further." She smiled and

Hannah looked away, trying to steady her breathing and pressing her lips together hard, feeling butterflies pour through her stomach as she did so. She waited for Lord Bentham to protest again, to tell Miss Hawkins that there was really no need for her to wait, only for him to clear his throat and then turn toward her with a smile. A smile that was somewhat awkward, pulling one side of his lips upward only, whilst his gaze slipped to her cheeks rather than meet her eyes.

"Shall we, Miss Seymour?" he asked, astonishing her entirely. "You have your lady's maid, I presume?"

Hannah swallowed her surprise and nodded, turning her head to beckon the lady's maid that was waiting to do her bidding. "But of course," she murmured, ignoring the beaming smile that settled on Miss Hawkins' face. "Where shall we begin, Lord Bentham?"

He hesitated, grimacing for a few moments as he considered, his shoulders sagging just a little.

"As much as it pains me to suggest it, I have wondered about the library," he admitted, and Hannah nodded encouragingly. "It has a great many books and whilst the staff have searched there, I do wonder if that is the room where things are most likely to have been missed."

"An excellent suggestion," Miss Hawkins responded, before Hannah could say anything. "I shall bring the others along when they return from their walk as I am sure we will need everyone to spend a good deal of time within that room to ensure every book is looked at. I do not think they will be long." With this, she smiled and stepped back, making to sit down quickly and then waving a hand so as to encourage both Hannah and Lord Bentham to commence. Lord Bentham cleared his throat and, to Hannah's surprise, offered her his arm, inclining his head as he did so. She stared at him, her heart pounding furiously, her skin prickling as she tentatively reached out and put her hand under his arm, swallowing hard when he smiled at her.

There is so much that has been broken, she told herself as they began to walk toward the door. *So much that has been shattered between us. Is there any possibility that now, somehow, we might find a way to put things back together again?*

"MIGHT you be able to answer a question, Miss Seymour?"

Hannah looked up into Lord Bentham's face as they walked into the library, feeling a prickle of anticipation run down her spine as she did so. "But of course," she said at once, dropping her hand from his arm as he turned to face her, a little surprised at the dark expression that now lingered on his features. "Is something the matter?"

Lord Bentham said nothing in response for a moment or two, looking at her but saying not a word. There were shimmers of silver in his dark blue eyes, like clouds forming above the sea, and Hannah felt herself drawn to them, just as she had been when they had first begun to know each other a little better.

"What is Miss Lewisham like?" he asked, the words falling on her like heavy stones, sending weight down into her soul. "If there is the possibility that I should have to marry her, then I should like to know her character."

Hannah turned away, wandering further into the room and throwing her response back to him over her shoulder. "I do not know her particularly well, Lord Bentham," she said softly. "But she appears to be a quiet young lady who possesses something of a strength within her character." She gave him a quick, tight smile and then looked back out toward the library, letting her gaze rove over the many, many books that were lying waiting for them.

"I see," Lord Bentham murmured, coming up behind her, his hand brushing her shoulder for a moment, forcing her to turn around and look up at him again. "And does she know anything of me?"

Hannah hesitated, remembering how shocked she had been when Miss Lewisham had first said Lord Bentham's name. "I have said nothing to her about you, if that is what you are asking, Lord Bentham," she answered slowly. "She does not think either overly well or overly poorly of you."

Lord Bentham dropped his head, his sigh ripping from his lips. "You are much too kind, Miss Seymour," he told her, slowly lifting his head, his expression quite downcast. "You have every right to express the truth of my character to whomever you wish and yet you choose not to do so. I cannot help but feel as though I do not deserve any such kindness from you."

"I suppose you do not," she answered wryly, before she could stop herself. "I will not pretend that I haven't found the last few weeks to be very difficult indeed."

Lord Bentham closed his eyes, lines forming around them as he squeezed them shut. "I did you a good deal of harm," he said regretfully. "I have been naught but selfish and unkind. I have said it a good many times before but I have no need to hide my guilt from myself or from you, Miss Seymour. You do not need to show kindness to me, for I am quite certain that I do not deserve it." He stepped away, leaving her to stand alone and watch him walk to the other side of the room, his shoulders slumped and his steps heavy.

The memory of what she had said to Miss Hawkins came back to her almost immediately, reminding her that she was struggling to know whether or not to trust Lord Bentham, to accept his words or the evident burden of his own guilt. And now, as she watched him pick up a book and shake it out, only to turn and pick up the next one, Hannah felt her heart swell with a sense of compassion. He had taken responsibility for his behavior and had not balked at the consequences that had followed. He had been entirely open and honest with her, confessing as though she were the only one who could save him. She wanted to believe him, she realized, turning around to begin searching through one shelf of books for the papers that he required. But if she *did* allow her heart to soften toward him, and allowed herself to believe his words and accept his apology, then was she not setting herself up for yet another injury by his hand? What if he pulled himself back just as she was falling in love with him for what would be the second time?

Sighing, Hannah continued to search through the shelf of books, her heart sinking as she looked up and realized just how many there were to look through. Glancing over her shoulder, she saw Lord Bentham pick something up, turning it over in his hand before pressing it back into the book he held in his other hand.

"Have you found something?"

He started, looking up at her with something akin to guilt.

"I have," Lord Bentham replied, sending a shiver of anticipation up Hannah's spine. "But it does not offer us any further hope, I confess."

"Oh?" She reached out and took what he offered her, turning it over in her hand. It was a thin piece of parchment, folded twice, with one edge gently pointing upwards. She looked up at him, curiosity building. "What is it?"

Lord Bentham shrugged, his eyes a little downcast. "I do not know," he said with a wave of his hand. "I do not think that there is anything of significance there."

She hesitated, then tugged it open gently. The parchment appeared to be a quite aged given the difficulty that came in unfolding it. When she did so, there appeared only two words written within.

"Lion Heart?" she repeated, looking up at Lord Bentham curiously. "What does that mean?"

Lord Bentham glanced back at her, before returning his gaze to the bookshelves, clearly eager to carry on searching. "I do not know. It must have been a note pressed into this book by someone some time ago."

Everything in Hannah held her back from agreeing, her brow furrowed as she looked down at the note again, her eyes darting back and forth over the written words. Something within her heart said that there was more to this than first met the eye.

"What book did you find it in?" she asked, making her way quickly across the room, toward the bookshelf that Lord Bentham had been searching. "Does it bear any significance?"

Lord Bentham frowned and hurried to join her. "I do not know," he said truthfully. "I have not looked at the books or their titles." Coming alongside her, he sorted through the books he had replaced on the shelves only to hesitate, pause, and then pull one out with a dark green cover and gold imprinted text on the spine.

"Is this it?" she asked, and Lord Bentham nodded, a line forming between his eyebrows as he frowned hard, turning the book over so as to look at the front cover again.

"I know this book," he said quietly, his eyes flashing with a sudden recognition. "It was one that my father purchased for me some years ago. I confess I have never read it." His eyes lowered to the book and he ran one hand over the cover, as though it brought him some sort of comfort to do so. "It is by a man called Defoe."

Hannah reached out and took the book from Lord Bentham, their fingers brushing as she did so. Sparks ran all up her arm, but she ignored them with an effort, turning the book over in her hand.

"'Captain Singleton'," she read aloud, realizing that she herself had read this. "Then this book is of significance."

"Indeed," Lord Bentham murmured, his eyes a little wide. "My father used to tease me that I should never read the book, even though he had purchased it for me. I would always reply that I had every intention of reading it but that I had not yet had the time to do so and would list the most ridiculous and foolish things that had taken up my time, as some sort of excuse." A sad smile captured his mouth and he held out his hand for the book again. "My father would laugh and we would share a few moments of joy together. In fact..." He trailed off, his breath hitching as he stared at her, as though something had only just begun to make sense to him. "When his will was read out, there was mention of this book."

Hannah's stomach tightened, her heart quickening. "What did it say?"

The corner of his mouth quirked, a wistful look in his eyes. "My father had added a note that stated that he hoped I would read his will with a good deal more accuracy and intention than I had ever read Defoe." A quiet chuckle left his lips, his eyes downcast but his smile still there. "I can remember how it brought me a little light in the midst of my grief."

There was such a swell of emotion in that particular moment that Hannah could not help but reach out and touch his hand. He looked at her in surprise but then his shoulders dropped and he pressed her fingers before she let go.

"Is there a possibility," Hannah began, thinking quickly, "that the remark made in the will was so that you would go to this book?" She watched Lord Bentham's expression closely, seeing his eyes flare and his mouth form an almost perfect circle. "Mayhap he hoped that you would discover this note long before now."

Breath rattled out of him as Lord Bentham closed his

eyes, no longer looking either wistful or happy. Instead, he appeared to be almost regretful, upset that he had not done as he ought.

"I do not mean to upset you or to suggest you have not done your duty in any way," she said quickly as she handed him back the book. "I merely wonder if the reason such a thing was noted in the will was that this note was placed here by your father for you to discover after his death. After all, would your late father have expected your mother to open and read this book?"

"No, he would not have," Lord Bentham replied quickly, his eyes darting to hers, the words beginning to tumble out of his mouth now. "My mother had her own shelves here, designated specifically for the books she wished to read." He thrust one arm out, pointing to the opposite side of the room. "Her books are kept over there."

"Then," Hannah said, excitement growing in her chest, "surely we must believe that this note was put here by your late father specifically for you, Lord Bentham. That it has been put here for an explicit reason, so that you might discover whatever it is that your father has set out for you."

Lord Bentham considered this, his eyes lingering on her face, his jaw tightening for just a moment. "It is something I ought to have understood and explored right away," he said heavily. "I feel as though I have failed in my duties, especially when I have very little understanding as to what that note might mean." He rubbed a hand across his eyes, clearly frustrated with himself. "And I should have discovered it much sooner than at this moment."

She put a hand on his arm as he held the book in both hands, fixing her eyes to his. "You were grieving for the loss of your father, Lord Bentham. It was a shock, from what I recall you have told me. Therefore, you must not take on such a burden of guilt when there is no need for you to do so." Pressing his hands, she held them tightly. "Have a little hope, Lord Bentham, and do not allow yourself to sink into despondency when there is no need to heap blame upon yourself." Heat traveled up her arms in waves, aware of how he looked at her, his eyes searching hers as though he might find some sort of hope within her expression. "This may be nothing at all or it may lead us to the answers we have been searching for." Her hand tightened on his arm, fire beginning to burn in her veins as her determination soared. "You may not know at present what such a note means, but if you allow it to run around your mind, to consider it carefully, I am sure that you will find an answer."

Lord Bentham said nothing in response, holding her gaze before, to her shock, he settled one hand over hers. Hannah's breathing quickened, suddenly aware that, aside from her maid who was, no doubt, now facing the other way, she was quite alone with Lord Bentham. It was as though nothing had ever occurred to separate them, nothing had ever happened to push them asunder, and in that moment, Hannah felt her heart lift with such happiness that it jolted her whole body.

Her hand pulled from his and she dropped her head, her face flushing as she turned her head away, not wanting him to see just how much a simple touch had affected her.

"Miss Seymour," Lord Bentham said, a little throatily. "I did not mean to embarrass you."

"You did not," she told him quickly, not turning back to look at him. "Now, this 'Lion Heart'." Finally, she managed to dart a quick glance back toward him. "Do you have lions within this house or in the grounds themselves?"

Lord Bentham frowned, then nodded. "There are some within the grounds, yes," he told her. "But there is nowhere for them to be hiding any sort of note, particularly not for years. They are stone sculptures, and do not have any place that would house a piece of parchment securely."

She nodded, looking absently around the room. "Then it must be elsewhere in the house," she said firmly. "I would surmise that, for the time being, Lord Bentham, we leave the search for these papers and instead concentrate on this note and where it might lead."

Smiling at her, Lord Bentham looked a good deal

more at ease than she had seen him in some time, the strain beginning to wipe itself away from his expression. She saw him as he had been at the first, when she had been introduced to him. He had been genuine in his manner, welcoming and amiable, without any suggestion that he might one day break her heart by choosing his own pleasures and his own selfishness over whatever she might offer him.

"You are a Shadow, Miss Seymour, and thus I shall bow to your instincts and intelligence," he told her, his compliments bringing a slight flush to her cheeks. "I would be glad to do whatever it is you ask of me."

"Good." She smiled at him in return, trying to keep her manner brisk. "Then we shall look for this 'Lion Heart', searching through each of the rooms just as we had intended at the first."

He looked at her steadily for a moment, then dropped his gaze to the floor. "And you will remain with me, Miss Seymour?" he asked, a little more quietly. "You are content to search through these rooms by my side?"

"I can see no reason why not," she answered brightly, not allowing her heart to flood with emotion as she glanced at him before making her way to the door. "Come, Lord Bentham, I think we should share with the other Shadows what we have discovered."

She made to pull the door open only to hear Lord Bentham call for her to wait. Turning her head, she was astonished when Lord Bentham bowed low in front of her, his obvious sign of respect and gratitude flooding her heart. She blinked in surprise as he lifted his head, seeing his hand outstretched and extending her own in return.

"I will not ask you to speak of what you do not wish to," he said quietly, his words spoken with great care, "but Lord Haddington stated that you yourself were in a situation of great trial and difficulty."

Hannah swallowed hard, a frisson of fear running straight through her, her stomach tightening and her smile fading completely. She did not want to talk about her own father, did not want to tell Lord Bentham the truth about what her father had threatened.

"I know a little of your father," Lord Bentham continued, his fingers pressing hers for a moment. "I am well aware of his reputation, and the way that he has a hold on almost every gentleman in London." His brows lowered and his eyes narrowed, making Hannah aware that he felt nothing but anger over the way her father conducted himself within society. When he spoke again, however, Lord Bentham's voice was measured and steady. "If there is anything that I can do to assist you in any way, then I would like to make it quite clear to you now, Miss Seymour, that I would be more than willing to do so. I have failed terribly, I know, but I swear to you that I will not do so again." He lifted her hand and brushed his lips over it, heat spiraling through her core and sending a wave of warmth over her skin. "You are so willing to help me, so kind in setting aside the past in order to assist Miss Lewisham as well as myself. I cannot understand it, but I am grateful for it, Miss Seymour. Truly, you are an astonishing creature and I cannot help but express my thankfulness, as well as repeat my sorrow and regret once again."

Hannah could say nothing, feeling the urge to step into his arms begin to grow within her, until it felt as though it would fill every part of her, rendering her quite unable to do anything other than that. Lord Bentham looked down into her eyes, his gaze warm but a shadow of regret still lingering there. How much she wanted to believe him. How desperately she wanted to trust him. And yet, Hannah knew that she could not let her emotions push all sense from her mind. She had to be careful, taking one step at a time until she knew precisely what the future held for Lord Bentham and Miss Lewisham, and until she herself was able to discover whether or not Lord Bentham's words of regret were completely genuine.

"Lord Bentham?" The sound of a loud voice reached their ears, shattering the moment between them. "Miss Seymour?"

Hannah turned at once and pulled open the door, her heart suddenly pounding furiously as Lady Catherine practically ran into her.

"Oh, thank goodness," she said, one hand on her

chest as she looked at Lord Bentham. "Lord Bentham, you must come at once."

"Why?" Hannah asked, unable to prevent herself. "Is something wrong?"

Lady Catherine shook her head. "No, nothing is wrong," she said quickly, "it is only that Lord Greene and Miss Lewisham have arrived earlier than expected and are just being shown into the drawing room at this present moment." She grasped Hannah's arm tightly. "Lord Bentham, you must take Lord Greene somewhere within the estate so that The Shadows can speak openly with Miss Lewisham and look at the ornament she has brought us. And we must do so at once, before your other guests arrive and there is less of an opportunity."

Lord Bentham moved quickly, not hesitating for even a moment. "At once," he said, striding down the hallway with quick steps. "Thank you, Lady Catherine. It seems we are about to become very busy indeed."

"Oh?" Lady Catherine looked at Hannah, a little confused. "What does he mean?"

"He refers to this," Hannah replied, holding out the note to her friend. "There is the chance that the late Lord Bentham has left a trail for his son to follow, although it may very well turn out to be nothing."

Lady Catherine smiled, her chest still heaving as she struggled to catch her breath. "But you do not think so."

"No," Hannah answered steadily. "I do not. I think this may lead us down a long, winding path that may end up tying everything together into one satisfactory conclusion."

Nodding, Lady Catherine took Hannah's arm and together, they began walking back toward the drawing room, taking their time so that Lady Catherine could catch her breath. "Let us hope so," Lady Catherine murmured, patting Hannah's arm with her free hand. "For it feels as though, with every step we take, this mystery only deepens."

"Miss Lewisham, Lord Greene," George said as he walked into the drawing room with both Lady Catherine and Miss Seymour just behind him. "How very good to see you both." Bowing, he waited until Miss Lewisham had risen from her curtsy before continuing, a little slighted that Lord Greene had only inclined his head rather than bowing as he ought. "I trust your journey was not particularly arduous? I believe your estate is only a little over a day's travel from here."

"We have made it, at least," Lord Greene muttered, looking around the drawing room with a distinctly unimpressed air. "I presume your other guests will be arriving soon?"

George, a little nonplussed by the gentleman's

evidently dismissive manner, took a moment to gather himself before he replied.

"Yes, they will be arriving a little later," he said, noting that Miss Lewisham would not look at him directly. "You are the first." He smiled as broadly as he could, seeing how Miss Seymour and Lady Catherine curtsied to Miss Lewisham before drawing her into a quiet conversation so that he might pull Lord Greene away. "Might I show you around the house, Lord Greene? Or would you prefer to rest after your journey?"

Lord Greene's eyes flashed as though George had said something quite insulting. "You would not prefer to wait for the rest of your guests?" he asked with a slight lift of one bushy eyebrow. "Or is it that you would prefer to spend time with my niece and thus, are seeking an opportunity to do so?"

George cleared his throat, aware that the other conversation had come to an almost immediate stop. He looked at Miss Lewisham for a moment, seeing the stricken expression on her face.

"I merely thought you might be interested in seeing the house that your niece will come to live in," he said, not looking at Miss Seymour as he spoke. "There are a few matters that we will need to discuss at some point." He shrugged. "Why not now?" He could easily make up some points to discuss with Lord Greene, be it the dowry that Miss Lewisham would bring or when and where their marriage ought to take place. He held Lord Greene's gaze firmly, not wanting him to even have a momentary suspicion that George was feigning what he now put forward.

"Very well," Lord Greene said after a long moment, and George practically felt the exhalation of relief that came from Miss Lewisham, although he did not even move as Lord Greene spoke.

"I am sure my niece would prefer to rest, however," Lord Greene continued, turning sharply toward Miss Lewisham. "Come, my dear." His tone was sickly sweet and held no true affection, nor did there come a smile to Miss Lewisham's face as she looked to her uncle. "Let me help you to your room."

Miss Seymour smiled and looped her arm through Miss Lewisham's before she could take a step forward toward her uncle. "You need not worry yourself, Lord Greene," she said in a bright and airy tone although George could see the thunderous clouds in her grey eyes. "We are well able to take care of Miss Lewisham. We are all so very glad to see her."

"Indeed," Miss Hawkins added, smiling just as warmly as Miss Seymour had done. "We shall ensure she receives some refreshment and thereafter, help settle your niece in her room if she requires a rest."

Lord Greene frowned, his eyes hooded. "I do not think—"

"Let me just ring the bell for tea," Lady Haddington said, cutting Lord Greene off completely. "And do sit down, Miss Lewisham, you must be quite weary after your journey. I am sure some tea will revive you and Lord Bentham has the most excellent of staff so it will be with you in a moment."

"Along with some wonderful cakes and the like," Lady Ann said, guiding Miss Lewisham to a chair and sitting down beside her. "Tell me, are you at all hungry? I am sure we could send for a little more than cake if you are."

Smiling inwardly and rather proud of all that the ladies had achieved in ensuring that Lord Greene was separated from his niece, George cleared his throat.

"Shall we leave the ladies to their own conversation?" he suggested, gesturing toward the door. "I am sure they will be able to take good care of Miss Lewisham." He did not wait for a response but rather quickened his steps toward the door, not pausing for Lord Greene to catch up with him. Stepping out into the hall, he slowed his steps until Lord Greene strode after him, clearly unable to do anything other than leave his niece in the drawing room, despite his obvious reluctance to do so. A sense of satisfaction rose in George's chest as he walked along the hallway, muttering some inane comments about the décor and the like. Lord Greene said nothing for some minutes, following George as they walked to the section of the estate which held all the portraits. It was some distance from the drawing room and with every step, George felt a little better. There was no way now for Lord Greene to turn around and hurry back to his niece, bursting into the room to discover her speaking of or even showing the ornament to the others. She would be quite safe.

"Ah, and this, I presume, was your late father."

George frowned, looking up at the portrait of his father and finding the way that Lord Greene was watching him with such intensity in his eyes rather unsettling. "Yes," he said, realizing that he had not looked at this picture for some time. The portrait was of his father sitting in his study, where he had almost always been, from what George recalled. His father had always had that air of strength and power within him, which seemed to practically radiate out from him no matter what time of day it had been. Even now, George could still feel that sense of respect from deep within himself, rising up as he looked at his father. His mind felt heavy with grief for a moment, half wishing that his father was still here, ready to give him advice.

"How strange that he never spoke to you of my niece," Lord Greene murmured, looking from the portrait to George and then back again. "Was it because he thought you unworthy of her, I wonder?"

George felt his hackles begin to rise but with an effort, pushed them back down again. Lord Greene was doing all he could to irritate and anger him and he did not want to permit the fellow to succeed. He did not understand the man's reason for doing so, although he supposed it came from an eager desire to wield some sort of power or control over George. He would choose not to react, to keep a hold of his temper, so that there could be nothing improper in his conduct.

"You have not found the papers?"

"No," George said stiffly, keeping his gaze fixed on the portrait. "I have not."

"Then I am afraid that I shall have to insist that, even without your father's seal, the marriage take place," Lord Greene said firmly. "The betrothal should be announced at your house party."

"You forget yourself, Lord Greene," George said, a flare of anger in his voice, his eyes narrowing and his hands tightening as he turned to face the gentleman. "This is *my* home and I shall take all the time I require to search for these papers. I want to be absolutely certain that such a thing was agreed to by my father before I take the next step."

Lord Greene did not seem to be even a little upset by George's irate tone, turning away from him and wandering along the hallway to look at some other portraits. "And just how long will I be expected to wait?" he said with a curl of his lip. "My niece will soon reach the day of her birth and as yet, no banns have been called." His eyes darkened, his stance a little intimidating as he pointed one long finger out toward George. "You intend to use this delay to find a way to remove yourself from her, do you not?"

"That is a gross misjudgment on your part!" George exclaimed angrily. "I have every right to pursue this so that I can be quite certain about it all. If the papers cannot be found after a certain length of time, then I will abide by the wishes set down by my father." A heavy weight settled in his stomach at such a statement, but he forced himself to continue. "No matter what happens, I can assure you, Lord Greene, that I am a man of honor."

"A man of honor?" Lord Greene spat, his mocking tone only adding fuel to George's fury. "A gentleman who will not say how long he will look for these papers, leaving my niece in a state of confusion and doubt?" He laughed harshly and George's lip curled, his hands fisted as he fought to keep a grip on his temper—a grip that was slowly loosening with every moment.

"I will not permit your niece to be left waiting," George threw back. "But you must understand—"

"Understand?" Lord Greene boomed, throwing his arms wide. "You are speaking of a young lady who has lost her father and now has only just discovered that the gentleman who is meant to marry her has decided it might not be what he wishes. She is in a dreadful state, uncertain what is to happen and fearful that you will turn your back on her and leave her alone and without purpose." He shook his head, looking angrily at George. "Her reputation will be ruined and she will most likely end her days as a spinster."

"That will not be my doing."

"The very least you can do," Lord Greene continued hotly, his expression darkening with every second, "is to tell her just how long you will search for these papers."

"I have no doubt that Miss Lewisham will understand just how—"

"Enough dithering, Lord Bentham." Lord Greene's voice grew louder and George's chest grew tight with anger. "Answer me, man!"

"I am attempting to do so, I—"

"Just how long do you expect her to wait?"

"If you would listen, I—"

Lord Greene bellowed furiously, "How long, Lord Bentham?"

"By the end of the week."

George froze, staring at Lord Greene and realizing, with a growing horror, what he had just said. Spurred on by the furious exclamations of Lord Greene, he had blurted out, in his frustration and anger, something that he had not had any intention of saying.

"Until the end of the week," Lord Greene repeated, his tone now silky smooth, a small smile tugging at the corner of his mouth. "That is acceptable, Lord Bentham." He cleared his throat and then gave a small shrug. "I think I shall rest for a short time, Lord Bentham. You will excuse me."

George could say nothing, awash with embarrassment and shame, realizing that Lord Greene had managed to manipulate him without any particular difficulty. No doubt, when he did not find the papers, Lord Greene would present his niece to George and insist that the arrangements begin. Banns would be called. The wedding would go ahead and he would never be able to extract himself from it.

And what of Miss Seymour?

George closed his eyes, feeling himself swaying just a little as he battled to regain some sense of calm. He had to believe that he would find these papers—and if not them, then the ornament—before the end of the house party. One way or another, he intended to free himself from this betrothal, so that he might propose to the only lady he now wished to stand beside him.

The thought had his eyes flaring wide, his breath catching in his chest as he realized what his desire now was. To be wed to Miss Seymour, to do what he ought to have done from the very beginning, seemed now to be the single, strongest desire deep within his heart. Everything that had occurred had knocked him back, had thrown him asunder, and had forced him to look at himself, just as he was. What he had been faced with had left a bitter taste. All he wanted now was to turn his back on what he had chosen in the past, in the desperate hope that Miss Seymour might offer him another opportunity, might believe that he could have undergone such a drastic change as had truly happened within him.

But now, such a thing might never happen, given

what he had just promised to Lord Greene. Rubbing one hand down his face, George turned back to the portraits, his eyes finding that of his father, looking at it for a long time as if he might be able to draw strength or clarity from it.

"I think you *would* be deeply ashamed of me, Father," he found himself saying, a heavy weight pushing down on his soul, feeling as though his father's stern gaze was still watching him, even though it was naught more than a work of art. "I have not made wise decisions of late. In fact, I am in such a confusion that I..."

He trailed off, his voice fading away to nothing as his eyes snagged on something within the portrait. Taking a small step closer, he narrowed his gaze, looking at the portrait with a good deal more intent.

In the background of the portrait, just behind his father's left shoulder, was a lion. It appeared to be standing on top of a wooden box of some kind, which had carved on the front of it the shape of a heart.

George blinked rapidly, his breathing shallow as he tried to work out where such a piece might be. He could not think, going over each room in his mind but finding nothing to catch his attention.

"You! You there." A footman moved closer as George beckoned him. "Livingston, is it not?"

The footman cleared his throat and inclined his head. "Yes, my lord."

"That." George jabbed at the portrait with one finger. "That, there. Do you know where it is?"

The footman leaned a little closer, but not before casting George a rather strange look. He looked at the lion, then at the portrait, and then at the lion again. "My lord?"

"The lion and the box," George said insistently, barely lifting his eyes from it. "Do you know where it is in the house?" Finally, he dragged his eyes back to the footman, seeing him frown. "Were you not present here at the time of my father?"

Livingston nodded, creasing his forehead as he considered "I was, my lord," he agreed quietly. "That was once in his study, I believe."

George turned to face him, his heart quickening again. "His study?" he repeated, his brows dropping low. "I do not recall it being present."

"Then, most likely, it was put into storage, my lord," the footman replied apologetically, as though it was his own doing. "Might I go and look for it for you?"

Shaking his head, George began to back away from the portrait. "No," he said, giving a wave of his hand. "Thank you. You are dismissed."

Turning on his heel, he found himself running down the hallway back toward the drawing room, one idea and one idea only resting on his mind. He had to tell The Shadows about the note he had discovered in the book and, thereafter, about the carved lion and wooden box that might themselves hold the papers related to his engagement. His breath came quickly as he burst into the room, six pairs of eyes turning toward him in astonishment. He tried to explain his sudden interruption, but his labored breathing forced him to put his hands on his knees, struggling to take in air.

"Lord Bentham," Miss Seymour said, moving a little closer to him and bending her head to look at him. "Are you all right? Where is Lord Greene?"

He looked up at her, his hands still on his knees, his lungs burning. "The lion heart, Miss Seymour," he gasped, seeing the flash of recognition in her eyes. "I think I know where it might be."

8

It took a few minutes for Hannah to explain what Lord Bentham meant, seeing the astonishment on each face as she did so, but noting with interest the relief that seemed to etch itself across Miss Lewisham's expression.

"We should go to look immediately," Lord Bentham cried, the moment she had finished. "It is of the greatest importance that we—"

Hannah held up one hand. "Whilst I would concur with you, Lord Bentham, I think it is also important for you to sit with Miss Lewisham for a time, so that you might see what she has brought with her, as well as ensuring that we make use of this time without Lord Greene present." She could see the eagerness in his eyes beginning to fade and found herself wanting to go with him immediately, but glancing back into the wide eyes of the white-faced Miss Lewisham, Hannah pushed aside her own desire and forced herself to encourage Lord Bentham to remain. "Come, Lord Bentham. I will go and look for this object later this evening and by myself, if I must."

Lord Bentham let out a long breath but nodded and followed her toward where Miss Lewisham was sitting. Much to Hannah's relief, Miss Lewisham rose almost at once, curtsying again as though she and Lord Bentham were meeting for the first time.

"Lord Bentham," Miss Lewisham said, a little breathlessly. "The ladies here have informed me that you yourself are not particularly willing to wed me." A tiny smile caught her lips as Lord Bentham inclined his head. "I know that we have met only once before, but my uncle has attempted to convince me, since that time, that you are more than a little eager to move forward with our marriage."

"Then I hope you are as relieved as I that it shall not be taking place," Lord Bentham replied, and Miss Lewisham nodded. "That is, provided I can find the papers and the ornament." His eyes drifted toward the small, white figure placed on the table next to Miss Lewisham. "Is that it?"

Hannah picked it up and handed it to Lord Bentham, again feeling that same familiar warmth rush up her arm as his fingers touched hers. From the way his eyes jerked up to hers, he felt the same as she and

Hannah was forced to step back and drop her gaze, praying that none of her friends would notice the redness in her cheeks.

"A very well-dressed gentleman, it seems," Lord Bentham murmured, turning the figure over in his hand. The figurine was a pale cream all over, but the detail of the gentleman's clothing was more than a little apparent. "But..." His brow lowered and he looked up at the others for a moment, his gaze roving over them as though he wanted to see the same puzzlement in their expression as was in his eyes. "He is rather heavy, is he not?"

Hannah frowned, having not noticed such a thing. "He is?" she asked, taking a small step forward to look at the figurine more closely. Lord Bentham turned the figure over in his hand, inspecting it carefully, whilst the other Shadows rose from their chairs and came to stand nearby.

"I had not noticed anything of the sort," Miss Lewisham said, sounding apologetic. "But I confess I do not know much about such things."

Lord Bentham's frown deepened. "Normally, such figures, given that they are made of delicate materials, do not weigh a great deal. However, this one..." He shook his head, looking at it again as though he might find some sort of clue hidden on the surface. "It appears to be quite weighted. In addition, I had expected there to be some sort of small hole to the base, but there is none." His eyes dropped to Hannah's for a moment, before looking back at the figurine. "It is not like anything I have seen before."

"Lord Bentham!"

Taken aback by the loud voice that flung itself through the drawing room, Lord Bentham dropped the figurine, which fell to the floor, hitting the edge of the table as it fell. Miss Lewisham let out a loud exclamation, whilst Lord Bentham himself turned around to greet one of his newly arrived house guests—a rather loud and flamboyant Lady Florence, wife to Viscount Florence, who had decided to enter without being announced. The other Shadows moved forward to greet the lady whilst Hannah dropped to her knees beside the figurine and the greatly horrified Miss Lewisham, who looked as though she might burst into floods of tears at any point.

"It will be easily fixed," she whispered, reaching to pick up the figurine, only to notice that the figurine had fallen into two pieces. Part of the legs and the feet, whilst still joined together, now lay on the carpet, and as she reached for the main part of the figure, Hannah realized, with a sudden chill running through her, that there was something hidden inside of it.

"Rise quickly, Miss Lewisham," she said, grasping the other part and pushing both pieces into her pocket. "Greet Lady Florence, then claim a need to rest for a time before dinner. I will accompany you and together, we can look at what we have discovered." She gave the lady a warm, encouraging smile as she got to her feet, aware of just how Miss Lewisham trembled. The fear that must now fill her Hannah well understood, knowing that she, too, felt the very same for her own father. Reaching out, she looped her hand through Miss Lewisham's arm and stepped forward, ready to greet Lady Florence and the rather shy and retiring Viscount Florence.

"WHAT CAN IT BE?"

Hannah let out a long, slow breath as she turned the top half of the figurine over in her hand, leaving the legs and the feet to one side. Her eyes narrowed as she tried to make out what the object was, her fingers reaching for it.

Miss Lewisham pressed her fingers to her lips as Hannah gave the item a tug, frowning hard as she realized that it was stuck completely. "Little wonder Lord Bentham thought this figure was heavier than it ought to be," she murmured, seeing that whatever was stuck inside had been set there, mixed with a clay-like material that had dried and become very hard. Lowering it back to the table, she let out a small sigh and looked ruefully up at Miss Lewisham.

"I think, Miss Lewisham, that we will have to smash

the figurine if we are to remove whatever is hidden inside."

Miss Lewisham's eyes flared with horror, her hand pressed to her mouth, but she did not immediately protest.

"I know that you do not want to," Hannah continued gently, "but I believe that it is the only way."

"But my uncle," Miss Lewisham whispered, her hand still at her mouth, muffling her words further. "What will he say if he discovers it is broken?" Her eyes filled. "My mother. I..."

Hannah reached out and settled a comforting hand on Miss Lewisham's arm. "I well understand your fear," she said, wishing she had the opportunity to share precisely why she had such a great understanding of it, but knowing now was not the right time. "But you must not allow it to rule you. I speak as much to myself as I do to you, Miss Lewisham, but if we leave it as it is, then we might never discover why your uncle is so desperate to find the other figurine."

"And my mother," Miss Lewisham whispered, a single tear tracking down her cheek. She swallowed hard, dropped her hands to her lap, and then nodded, pressing her lips together for a moment so as to steady herself. "Yes, you are quite right, Miss Seymour." Her breath rattled out of her, but she did not step back from what she had said. "Please, continue."

Hannah gave her a quick smile and then turned her

attention back to the figurine, wondering who had put such great time and effort into hiding something within the depths of a gentleman figurine—and why they had done so. "You are doing very well, Miss Lewisham," she murmured, examining the figurine carefully. "No other guests know of your difficulties with your uncle, save for those whom you have told." Her eyes darted up to Miss Lewisham's for just a moment before moving back to the figurine. She frowned, thinking that they were going to have to smash it into pieces entirely but having very little idea of how to go about it.

"Could we pry it off?" Miss Lewisham asked, her voice sounding a little stronger now. "And might we then take out what is inside?"

Hannah frowned, trying to do so but finding that nothing would move. Her fingers began to pain her and so she stopped, shaking her head. "We could drop it again," she suggested, looking up at Miss Lewisham. "The reason it cracked and broke initially was because it hit the corner of the table before it reached the floor."

Miss Lewisham nodded, her eyes drifting around the room. "The fireplace?" she suggested as Hannah rose to her feet. "I can see no other place within your bedchamber where we might drop it onto a hard surface."

"Indeed." Hannah felt a tremor of excitement run through her as she held the figurine high in the air, and Miss Lewisham stepped back. Holding it tightly in her hands, she flung it down hard, stepping back with an exclamation as the figurine smashed hard against the fireplace. White pieces flew everywhere and, much to Hannah's relief, she found that the rest of the figurine was now in pieces, with the object in the middle of it now freed.

"What is it?" Miss Lewisham whispered, taking a tentative step forward. "Can you see it?"

Bending down, Hannah picked up what appeared to be a small metal key. There were a few pieces of clay stuck to it still and she cleaned them off carefully, stepping away from the smashed object and coming near to Miss Lewisham.

"A key," she said, wonder in her eyes. "I can hardly believe it."

Miss Lewisham took it from her, her eyes wide with bewilderment. "Why would someone hide a key within a figurine?" she asked softly, barely glancing up at Hannah as she held the key up to the light. "It is so small; I can hardly imagine what it might fit."

Hannah nodded. The key was shorter than her smallest finger yet still felt fairly robust. Taking it from Miss Lewisham again, she shook her head, having very little idea as to what it could open.

"We will have to show it to Lord Bentham just as soon as possible," she said, wondering how they were to have even a spare moment to show him what they had discovered. Her eyes lit up as a sudden idea took hold of her. "Mayhap the other figurine holds another key," she said as Miss Lewisham's eyes rose to hers. "And they both open something of great significance."

Miss Lewisham shook her head. "I could not say," she replied, a slight tremor to her voice. "My fear, at present, is what my uncle will say if he discovers that the figurine is smashed and broken beyond repair."

Hannah smiled and reached out to squeeze Miss Lewisham's hand. "You need not fear, Miss Lewisham," she said firmly. "If he enquires after it, simply tell him that you have left it in a safe and secure place within your room. I highly doubt he will attempt to go and search for it."

Miss Lewisham shuddered. "You do not know my uncle."

"I may not know him particularly well," Hannah responded swiftly, "but I assure you, Miss Lewisham, I am fully aware of the sort of gentleman Lord Greene is, for my own father has a very similar nature." She saw Miss Lewisham's eyes widen and gave her a rueful smile. "The reason I can assure you that he will not come and search your room for this item is simply because he will not expect you to behave in any other way aside from what he expects." Her smile grew steadily, a heaviness settling within her soul. "My own father does not know that I am a part of The Shadows, nor does he think that I have any other intention than to return to him once this house party has come to an end."

Miss Lewisham blinked in surprise, a faint spot of color in each cheek. "You do not intend to do so?"

Hannah let out a slow breath, considering. She had not quite decided what she ought to do, still finding herself to be rather afraid of the consequences of doing something other than what Lord Addington demanded, but knowing that to return would mean to bind herself to whichever odious gentleman her father had chosen for her.

"I do not want to go back," she told Miss Lewisham honestly. "My father does not have good intentions for my future and Lady Haddington has made it quite clear I am welcome to go and reside with her for a time, until I can find another way to escape from my father entirely." She drew in a long breath, settling her shoulders and lifting her chin. "And, Miss Lewisham, my intention now, should it come to it, is to do precisely that."

HANNAH COULD SEE the strain on Lord Bentham's face as he sat through yet another song by Lady Florence, although, aside from him, Lady Florence had a very attentive audience. Hannah was also rather surprised to notice that Lord Kerr—a gentleman she had only been introduced to this evening, upon his arrival—was in deep conversation with Miss Lewisham, sitting beside her on a couch and laughing at something she was saying. She could not help but smile at this, seeing the flush on Miss Lewisham's cheeks and finding her heart rather glad for her new friend. Lord Greene would never have permitted such a conversation to go on, of course, but Lord Paxton, Lord Haddington, and Lord Bentham had plied the gentleman with a good deal of port over dinner and now, much to Miss Lewisham's quiet delight, Lord Greene was sitting quietly in the corner, his head on his chest, giving every appearance of being asleep.

Looking around the drawing room, Hannah felt herself rather glad that she had decided to attend. The other Shadows were present, of course, and seemed to be enjoying their evening despite the weight of the mystery that was on each of their minds. She smiled softly as she saw Lady Haddington laugh up into Lord Haddington's eyes, finding a sudden swell of eagerness within her own heart that she might find something just as wonderful as they had done.

Sighing to herself, she continued to let her gaze drift around the room as, with a good many curtsies and smiles, Lady Florence stepped away from the pianoforte and allowed another young lady to step forward to the front.

"Miss Seymour, I could not help but come over to speak to you."

She started in surprise, half turning her head to see Lord Bentham coming to sit by her, his blue eyes swirling with both curiosity and unease.

"Lord Bentham," she said softly, her heart already quickening at his sudden nearness. "How have you fared this afternoon?"

He sighed and rolled his eyes, making her laugh. "I have not been as attentive to my guests as I might have been," he confessed. "My mind has been entirely settled on finding that wooden box and lion. I have been desperate to go into the attic to search for it, but I know that I could not do so given that I would return in a rather dusty fashion."

Another quiet laugh escaped her and, as she smiled, she saw a flash of happiness sparkle in Lord Bentham's eyes, even if it was for just a moment.

"You took the figurine from the room," Lord Bentham continued as the new performer began to sing and play the pianoforte. "It is safe, I hope?"

Searching his face, Hannah hesitated, wondering how best to explain what had occurred. "When you dropped the figure, Lord Bentham, it hit the edge of the table and thus, part of it separated from the other." Seeing him about to exclaim, his eyes wide with upset, she reached out and touched his hand, stopping his words from leaving his lips. "But it is good that such a thing occurred, Lord Bentham," she assured him brightly. "Miss Lewisham and I discovered something within."

He blinked, his mouth closing and his brows lifting. Hannah glanced toward the other side of the room and made certain that Lord Greene could not see her, before surreptitiously pulling the key from her pocket. She and Miss Lewisham had tied it with a lavender ribbon, leaving a large loop for Hannah to pull it into her hand. In one swift movement, she pressed it into Lord Bentham's hand, seeing the startled expression that jumped onto his face almost immediately.

"This key was within the figurine," she said, keeping her voice low. "Miss Lewisham and I were most astonished."

Lord Bentham took a few moments to glance down at his hand, his eyes wide as he took in what was now held there. With a deep breath, he closed his hand again tightly, before reaching over to touch his fingers to hers, pressing the key back into her palm. Hannah took it just as quickly as she could, pressing it back into the pocket of her gown and refusing to allow the flurries of excitement and heat that rushed through her at his touch to affect her manner or behavior in any way.

"This mystery continues to grow," Lord Bentham muttered, lines forming around his eyes as he frowned hard. "We already know that Lord Greene is eager to find both of these figurines." His eyes looked back into her own. "What does the second one contain, do you think?"

"I do not know," Hannah conceded. "Another key, mayhap? Perhaps he needs both to open something of great importance."

Lord Bentham nodded slowly, his eyes shifting from here to there as he sat beside her, wordlessly. Hannah said nothing, aware that he was thinking through all that she had revealed to him and wanting to give him that time to do so.

After a few minutes, Lord Bentham let out a long breath, his eyes focused on Hannah again as he allowed himself a small smile.

"I must still find this lion," he told her. "And we must gather The Shadows so as to tell them about this development."

"And we must still search for the figurine," she added, a tug of concern in her heart. "I must tell you, Lord Bentham, that the gentleman figure is now quite broken and entirely beyond repair." She gave a small shake of her head. "Miss Lewisham is quite distressed, afraid of what her uncle will do should he discover it—and, of course, very upset as regards her mother's situation." An idea struck her and without meaning to, she clutched at his hand, unaware that Miss Hawkins and Lady Ann, who were sitting opposite, had noticed her quiet conversation with Lord Bentham. "Might we not send someone to bring her here?"

Lord Bentham began to shake his head, only to stop himself, his lips twisting and a dark look entering his eyes. "It grieves me to hear that Lord Greene has treated his sister-in-law in such a fashion, and that he is using her suffering to force his niece's hand," he said heavily.

"I would go to the Dower house myself, but..." He gestured to the rest of the guests as Hannah, aware now of the quick glances being sent in her direction from her two friends, pulled her hand back, her face hot.

"Do you think Lord Paxton and Lord Haddington would go to the Dower house?" he asked abruptly, his eyes suddenly bright. "They could make some pretense of some sort, I am sure, to ensure that Lady Greene is brought here safely and securely."

"They would have to pretend that Lord Greene had sent them," Hannah replied quietly, her heart thumping hard against her chest. "They would have enough bluster and enough of a presence to force the staff to do as they asked, however, surely?" Hannah knew very well that most of the servants would do the bidding of their master without question, and certainly would obey his guests and make no complaint about it—but to go against the strict instructions of their master in the face of two complete strangers coming to the house was an entirely different situation.

Lord Bentham nodded slowly, a brightness in his expression that made Hannah smile in return.

"I think they would be able to force their way in if they had to," he said with a wry grin. "But I am sure they would be able to do it. And how glad Miss Lewisham would be to know that her mother is safe." His chest tightened. "And it might present us with an opportunity to demand that Lord Greene tell us precisely what he knows about these figurines, even if we do not manage to find the other in time." Biting his lip for a moment, he nodded to himself, clearly thinking things through. "With the shock of being presented with his sister-in-law and the rest of us standing by her, he may lose some of his conceit."

"Indeed," Hannah agreed, her heart gladdening as she saw the happiness in his eyes over what relief he could bring Miss Lewisham. This would help Miss Lewisham immensely, she knew, and with Lady Greene present, there might be an opportunity for them all to confront Lord Greene about all that he had done.

"How long will it take?" she asked, and Lord Bentham frowned. "Will they be able to bring her back in time for the end of the house party?"

Lord Bentham nodded, looking all about him. "If they leave this evening, then yes, I should think so," he murmured, making to rise to his feet, before sitting back down and looking at her again. "Will you linger, Miss Seymour? You will not retire, I hope, for there are still some other matters that we need to discuss."

"The lion's heart?" she asked, seeing him smile. "Yes, of course, Lord Bentham. I will not retire until we have had an opportunity to further our discussions."

"I thank you." The look in his eyes had her heart skipping a beat and she dropped her gaze, only to raise it again when he stepped away. Within a moment, Lady Ann and Miss Hawkins had hurried over to join her, their eyes fixed on hers, eager to hear of all that had passed between her and Lord Bentham. Hannah found herself laughing as she waved her friends' questions away, finding herself beginning to fill with happiness rather than any sort of despondency or sadness. It was all quite refreshing and she settled back in her seat, ready to listen to the next young lady's performance and waiting for Lord Bentham's swift return.

9

"I cannot thank you enough."

George smiled with satisfaction as Lord Paxton and Lord Haddington each bowed to Miss Lewisham, feeling contented that, at the very least, Lady Greene would be able to speak with openness and honesty to them all about what her brother-in-law had been doing the last few weeks. He had no right to demand that she linger, of course, not when Lord Greene was the one who had authority over his own family, but he doubted that Lord Greene's arrogance and supercilious attitude would remain when faced with The Shadows, Lord Haddington, Lord Paxton, and Lady Greene. He knew that Miss Seymour was encouraging Miss Lewisham to have a little more courage, to speak more openly, and to find a little more strength when it came to her uncle and he could only pray that she would be successful. They had three days now to find the figurine and the papers, three days before Lord Paxton and Lord Haddington returned with, they hoped, Lady Greene by their side. Miss Lewisham had been a little concerned that her mother would refuse to return with Lord Haddington out of fear of what her brother-in-law would do or say, but Lady Haddington had insisted that Lord Haddington would do all he could to encourage her, to the point of offering her residence with them should she be turned away from her brother's estate. George had marveled at Lady Haddington's generosity and kind spirit, feeling a deepening sense of shame within his own heart that he was not as she was.

"And now, we return to this note," Lady Catherine said as Lord Haddington and Lord Paxton quit the room. "Your 'Lion Heart'?" She sat back down in her chair and looked at George with a quizzical eye. "You believe you have found it?"

"I think I might know where it is and what it refers to," George said, having only just finished explaining all that had occurred that day. "The footman believes it has been stored in an attic somewhere, and thus, I have no other choice but to go and search for it."

Lady Ann nodded and reached for her cup of cooling tea. Even though it was by now the early hours of the morning, Lady Ann did not have the appearance of someone eager to retire to bed, just as none of the others did. Miss Seymour, he noted, was just as bright-eyed as she had been some hours ago, without a single evidence of weariness on her face. She was, he considered, quite magnificent.

"Then, should we not take this opportunity to go and search?" Miss Seymour asked briskly. "I am aware that the hour is late and that is it quite dark, but surely now—"

"I cannot think that to go searching about in the darkness would be wise," Lady Catherine interrupted, although her eyes darted down toward her beautiful cream gown, a note of worry in her voice. "Surely it would be best to wait until the morning, so that we might see a little more?"

"You have already been in the attic," Lady Ann reminded her pointedly, "and reappeared looking very dusty indeed." She laughed and George could not help but grin. "Is that why you do not wish to go again?"

Lady Catherine's face immediately went a very deep shade of red and she began to stammer, only for the rest of the group to erupt into laughter, until Lady Catherine herself began to laugh.

"The attic *is* dark, I will confess," George said, when a little more peace had been restored. "But it does not gain a lot of light during the day either." He lifted one shoulder, not wanting to demand that the others do as he requested but feeling a growing sense of urgency deep within him. "I would prefer to look for the wooden box and the lion as soon as possible, but I—"

"I am more than content to go with you," Miss Seymour interrupted, rising to her feet. "We will take candles, I presume?"

George opened his mouth to agree, only for Miss Hawkins to rise and move toward the mantlepiece, taking a candle from there. Lady Ann smiled and stood up, glancing down at her gown but then shrugging.

"If we are to get dusty, then dusty we shall be," she said firmly. "Now, which way should we go, Lord Bentham? I feel quite excited at the thought of finding this lion and seeing just what his heart contains."

As much as he did not want to admit it, there was something about being in the attic when the rest of the house was asleep that unsettled George. Even with the candles each of them held, he felt his heart beating a little more quickly, his stomach tight with nervousness that he did not want to feel.

"What should we do?" Lady Ann asked, her voice muted as though she did not want the objects in the attic to hear her. "There are a good few dust sheets on larger items and I would think that—"

"We can leave them be," Miss Hawkins interrupted,

her voice seeming louder in comparison to Lady Ann. "For the time being, at least."

"I would agree," George said, holding his candle aloft. "The attic is large, but we need not look under sheets at present."

Miss Seymour sneezed delicately and George chuckled, turning to glance back at her. "It is rather dusty in here and the less we disturb, the better."

"I could not agree more," Miss Seymour answered, rather thickly. "Now, shall we begin our search?"

George nodded and within a few minutes, they had all spread out across the attic, searching for the one thing that might lead them to their next clue. George pulled his thoughts away from Miss Seymour and began to look carefully, focusing his eyes on each object to make certain he had taken in precisely what was there. He did not know how long it was that they searched, for there came very little sound save for his own breathing and the occasional echoing footfalls from somewhere within the attic.

"Have you found anything yet?"

He turned, seeing Miss Seymour's face illuminated by the flickering candle she held in her hand. "No, not as yet," he said, feeling his heart turn over in his chest at the vividness of her gray eyes that seemed to sparkle with silver as she smiled at him. "You have not found anything either?"

She shook her head, her smile disappearing. "No.

Nothing." For a moment, she looked a little afraid and he put his hand out to her, resting it lightly on her shoulder. Miss Seymour glanced at him then looked away. "Forgive me, Lord Bentham," she murmured. "I feel such anticipation and then, when we find nothing, I feel a great disappointment and, from that, comes my fear."

"What do you fear, Miss Seymour?"

Her eyes met his and he felt her sigh, her shoulders dropping under his hand. "I fear that there will be no resolution," she said quietly, the candle flickering a little more from her exhalation of breath. "I fear that even with Lady Greene present, we will find nothing and Lord Greene will somehow achieve success in everything."

"He will not," George said firmly, pressing Miss Seymour's shoulder gently. "I will not allow it."

Miss Seymour nodded, blinked, and looked away, giving him the impression that there was something else she wanted to say but had chosen not to do so. George cleared his throat, looking keenly into her face until finally, she met his eyes.

"I do not have any intention of allowing the betrothal to continue," he said softly, taking a small step closer. "I do not want you to think that such a thing will happen, Miss Seymour." He did not know if he ought to continue, particularly not when there were two others of The Shadows present in the attic somewhere, but found that he could not help it. "I know that I have made grievous mistakes, Miss Seymour. I have treated you without consideration. I have been selfish. I have been foolish. And yet you have looked at me and decided that, in spite of what I have done, you would be willing to help me. You are the most extraordinary lady I have ever had the pleasure of knowing, and I must hope that, should there be an opportunity for me to seek a nearness with you again—even though I have already thrown it aside in my folly—you might, at the very least, consider it."

Her hand reached up and touched his, and he realized that she had moved all the closer to him, her fingers running across his hand. "You need have no doubt, Lord Bentham. I will do more than consider it." Her smile sent a flame into her eyes, his heart thumping furiously as he began to lower his head, realizing what he wanted to do but uncertain as to whether or not it was what he ought to do or what she would want.

"I would accept without hesitation," she murmured, her breath whispering across his cheek. "A good deal has occurred these last few days and yet, despite that, my heart has begun to heal from its hurt."

"I will do all I can to try and prove myself to you," he whispered, his free hand reaching up to brush gently across her cheek, aware of just how quickly his heart was beating, how strong the urge was to pull her into his arms. "Miss Seymour, I—"

"I have found it!"

A loud exclamation from another part of the attic had Miss Seymour stepping back from him, her heart turning and her feet moving away from him almost at once. George took a breath, giving himself a slight shake as he tried to gather himself. He had been so close to something, something momentous, and to have it pulled away from him in just a moment was rather startling.

"Lord Bentham!" Lady Ann cried, her candle a glimmer in the gloom as she came toward him. "Is this it?" She beckoned to him and he picked up his candle from where it sat and moved toward her, feeling a sudden thrill of anticipation running up his spine.

Within moments, he was looking at the very object he had seen in his father's portrait. The wooden carved lion sat atop the wooden box, which had a heart carved into the front of it. Bending down, he set his candle down carefully and ran his hands lightly over the box. There was a clear join where the lid would lift but try as he might, he could not do so.

"Well done, Lady Ann, Miss Hawkins," he said softly as his fingers traced the wooden carving. "Now, there must be a catch somewhere, some way for this to be opened."

"We could not find a way to lift the lid," Miss Hawkins stated as he grimaced.

There came nothing but silence as he tried to find something that would help him raise the lid, but he could find nothing. Frustrated, he rose to his feet and shook his head. "I cannot find a way."

Miss Seymour touched his hand. "Lord Bentham, if you recall, the note mentioned 'Lion Heart'." Coming to stand beside him, she glanced up into his face and then back to the lion box. "If we press the heart, mayhap we will..." She bent down and did just as she had suggested, the others watching her carefully. George held his breath, nothing but silence brushing over them all—until, finally, there came a small click.

Miss Seymour caught her breath, glancing up at him and then back to the box. The lid with the lion lifted and George leaned forward, trying to see what was within.

"Lord Bentham."

Turning, Miss Seymour handed him something small and folded, and he reached out to take it as she rose.

"Another note?" Miss Hawkins asked as The Shadows crowded around him, looking at the note in his hand. Handing his candle to Lady Ann, he unfolded the note, clearing his throat as he did so.

"My father clearly had a reason to send me to various places in this house, in order to find whatever it is he has hidden," he muttered, handing the note to Miss Seymour. "This note is just another object in the house, I believe."

"'A Golden Vase'," Miss Seymour murmured,

looking up at him with a frown. "Do you know what that is?"

"I believe I do," he said with a swell of relief in his chest. "But we should wait until the morrow to look at it. It is late enough already." Smiling broadly, he saw Miss Seymour looking at him, an excitement in her eyes as she smiled back at him.

"Well, I for one am very glad that it has been discovered," Lady Ann said with a laugh as she looked down at her gown. "I do not think I shall be anywhere near as dusty as Catherine was, which is something of a relief."

"Indeed," Miss Hawkins replied with a chuckle of her own. "Now, shall we?"

She began to walk toward the door, with Lady Ann following her. George hesitated, seeing Miss Seymour still standing by him, aware that there was a good deal more that needed to be said between them and yet struggling to find the words to express it.

"Might I come with you when you find this 'golden vase', Lord Bentham?" Miss Seymour asked as the footsteps of the others faded away. "I would very much like to see what is within."

Giving her a quick smile, he reached out for her hand, which, after a moment, she gave him. Lifting it to his lips, he kissed the back of her hand gently, wishing he could find a way to express all that he felt in this moment. "Miss Seymour, I would very much like it if you would continue on in this mystery by my side, leading the way, in fact, as you have always been."

Her smile was tender, her eyes swirling with sparks of silver. She said nothing but there was so much in her expression that he could already see all that she wanted to say.

"We should go," he said, forcing himself to step back from her before he did what he knew he wanted desperately to do. "Let us hope that tomorrow, we will be able to find the answer to all of this." He offered her his arm and she took it, looking up at him with a sense of gratitude in her face.

"Thank you," she said softly. "I look forward to tomorrow, Lord Bentham, in the hope that it will bring us all that we need."

10

<hr>

The golden vase.

Hannah could not stop thinking about all that had occurred last evening with Lord Bentham. Her heart beat a little more quickly with every thought of him, her hope beginning to burn brighter than ever before. She did not know what to think, but given how he had looked into her eyes and dropped a gentle kiss on the back of her hand, Hannah found herself wanting to believe that he felt something real for her now. There was the desire within herself to bring forgiveness to him, to forget about what had gone before so that she might find a way to step forward in renewed hope, and that desire was now slowly overcoming her fears. If she allowed herself to feel such things, then she might very soon discover a heart that was filled with a deep, roaring affection for Lord Bentham, unable to hide such a regard from even herself for much longer.

"Miss Seymour?"

Hannah looked up and smiled, making to rise to her feet to greet Miss Lewisham, only for the lady to wave a hand and smile, even though her smile was a little tight.

"Miss Lewisham, good morning," Hannah said, watching as the lady sat down opposite her at the breakfast table. "I hope you slept well." She watched the young lady as she reached to pour herself a cup of tea, noting the dark circles under her eyes and the paleness of her cheeks. Wanting to encourage her, Hannah continued to speak. "Last evening, Lord Bentham, Miss Hawkins, Lady Ann, and I discovered the whereabouts of the wooden lion and the chest it sat upon." Smiling at Miss Lewisham, who lifted her head sharply, Hannah let out a small, contented sigh, feeling the anticipation filling her for what might now soon occur. "We are to seek 'A Golden Vase', but Lord Bentham has stated that he knows precisely where such an item is." Closing her eyes for just a moment, she drew in a steadying breath in an attempt to take a hold of the sudden swell of excited anticipation that filled her. "This might all be over very soon, Miss Lewisham."

"Miss Seymour." Miss Lewisham's voice was shaking. There was no smile upon her face and her eyes held a look of terror, as though she was truly fearful about what was to come. "Miss Seymour, I fear that I must seek your help."

A frown flickered over Hannah's brow but she held the lady's gaze steadily. "But of course," she said slowly, wondering what it was now that troubled the lady so. "Is there something wrong?"

Miss Lewisham took in a long breath, letting it out slowly and then dropping her gaze to the table. "What if I am not present when the truth is discovered?"

Hannah's frown grew steadily darker. "What do you mean?"

Miss Lewisham lifted her tea and took a long sip, making Hannah aware of the fact that the lady was trembling. Her heart began to quicken with concern and she leaned forward in her chair, silently praying that no one else would enter the room to discover them. "Miss Lewisham?" she pressed, looking at the lady with a steadiness that seemed to encourage Miss Lewisham somewhat. "Tell me what you mean. Has your uncle threatened you?"

"No." Miss Lewisham put one hand over her eyes and let out a shaking breath. "No, Miss Seymour, he has not. Rather..." Her hand dropped and her tear-filled eyes looked back at Hannah desperately. "Rather, Lord Kerr has suggested that we might elope."

Hannah's mouth swung open and she stared at the lady for a long moment, unable to find any sort of reply or retort that she might make in order to express the shock that now ran through her.

"I do not know the gentleman very well at all, of course," Miss Lewisham continued, stammering a little, "but I have found myself telling him the truth about my uncle and he has now decided that he wishes to marry me and that the only way to do so is to elope."

Hannah shook her head firmly, panic striking her heart. "You should not do such a thing, Miss Lewisham."

"Why not?" There was a note of steel in Miss Lewisham's voice now, an anger that came from deep within herself as she held Hannah's gaze. "He is an excellent gentleman and you know very well that I do not wish to marry Lord Bentham." A sharpness came into her eyes that startled Hannah all the more. "I would have thought you, Miss Seymour, would not wish for me to do so either."

A retort came to Hannah's lips, but she held it back with an effort. Clearly, Miss Lewisham was in a state of desperation and she herself had to find a way to respond with consideration and kindness. Taking a few moments, she let out a long breath and then tried to speak carefully and slowly.

"Miss Lewisham, if Lord Kerr has offered to marry you, then I am glad for you," she said soothingly. "But to run away now, when the conclusion of the matter is only just before us, would not be wise." With a gentle smile, she tried to make Miss Lewisham see that there would only come more difficulty should she do such a thing, but Miss Lewisham's face held nothing but frustration. "Your uncle will soon see that he has not been successful," she continued, speaking a little more quickly now. "Your mother is to be brought here, and Lady Haddington has already offered to take you both to reside with her for a time, until—"

"My uncle will never allow us to depart," Miss Lewisham said, her voice dulled and her expression resigned. "My only hope is to either marry Lord Bentham so that my mother and I are kept from my uncle's cruelty, or to find another situation where I might be content."

Hannah closed her eyes and nodded slowly, fearful that the young lady was about to run into a situation without due consideration and yet understanding her reasons for doing so.

"Then," she said softly, "might I suggest, Miss Lewisham, that you ask Lord Kerr to tarry for only a short while?" Opening her eyes, she saw the guarded look begin to fall from Miss Lewisham's expression, leaving her a little more open than before. "I can see the fear, the frustration, the anger, and the desperation within your heart, Miss Lewisham, and I well understand it." Clearing her throat, she waved one hand about for a moment. "When matters with your uncle and the figurines are brought to a conclusion—which I think will happen tomorrow, if not before—then there will still be a day or so of the house party remaining. You will know the truth of it all by then. Your uncle will, as you have said, refuse to allow you and your mother to remain anywhere other than by his side, in which case—"

"I take my mother with me when we go to Scotland," Miss Lewisham breathed, her eyes suddenly sparkling with a fresh hope that Hannah could only smile at. "I understand what you mean now, Miss Seymour."

Hannah held her gaze. "I do hope that Lord Kerr is worthy of you, Miss Lewisham," she declared, trying to frame her concerns in as gentle a manner as possible. "He is friends with Lord Bentham, is he not?"

Miss Lewisham's expression softened all the more and Hannah was surprised at the look of affection that came into the lady's eyes. Could she really have struck up such a bond with the fellow so quickly?

"He is, yes," Miss Lewisham told her. "And he is gone to speak to Lord Bentham this very morning."

"I see," Hannah murmured, all the more astonished. "Then let us hope Lord Bentham gives him much the same advice, Miss Lewisham. And," she continued, her smile now one of hope, "let us pray that you will find the happiness you well deserve, with no difficulties or troubles to chase you any longer."

IT WAS NOT until the evening that Lord Bentham approached Hannah to speak to her quietly. They had spent the day with the rest of the guests, ensuring that the house party went well and that Lord Bentham played his part as host without any difficulties. The day had been fine and the gentlemen had gone to hunt and shoot in the afternoon, whilst the ladies had taken a picnic out of doors, with some choosing to remain inside so that they might not damage their delicate complexion. It had given The Shadows time to discuss Miss Lewisham's latest plans, with Lady Haddington telling them all that, according to Lord Haddington, Lord Bentham had been utterly astonished to hear such news from Lord Kerr and had been required to sit down hard for some minutes before he could allow himself to believe it.

"Lord Bentham," she murmured as some couples rose to dance together, with Lady Catherine playing the pianoforte for them all. "How do you fare this evening?"

He smiled at her. "All the better since I am now in your company," he told her softly. "I hear you spoke to Miss Lewisham today."

"And I hear you spoke to Lord Kerr," she replied, and he chuckled. "I was rather astonished."

"As was I," he admitted with a rueful look. "But I must admit, it is the fact that I was so very astonished that encouraged my heart to trust Lord Kerr's intentions." He shook his head again, as if he still could not quite accept what his friend had said. "But I did ask him to wait until the matter here had been brought to a conclusion. And so that his heart has a little more time to consider whether or not this is truly what he wishes."

Hannah smiled up at him. "I am glad to hear such a thing," she said honestly. "When do you think we might go in search of this golden vase?"

Lord Bentham glanced about him, smiled, and then shrugged. "Now?" he suggested, as she looked over his shoulder, seeing how the rest of the guests seemed to be enjoying themselves immensely, no longer requiring the presence of their host. "I can ask for Lady Ann or Miss Hawkins to join us."

"There is no need," Hannah found herself saying, stepping outside the bounds of propriety with evident ease, even though she knew full well she ought not to do so. "It will not take us long."

Lord Bentham considered this, then nodded. "Wait for just a moment, if you please," he murmured, then stepped away from her. Hannah watched as he spoke to Miss Hawkins for a moment, who nodded and then glanced toward her. Within a few moments, Lord Bentham had returned and gestured for her to quit the room, muttering that he would follow within a few moments.

"I asked Miss Hawkins to have The Shadows and Miss Lewisham brought to the library in a quarter of an hour," Lord Bentham said as he hurried along the hallway, with Hannah trying desperately to keep pace with him. "I have been unable to get into this room to find 'The Golden Vase' but I know I will be able to do so now, given that the rest of the guests are dancing."

"What room is it?" Hannah asked, only for Lord Bentham to come to a stop, push open a door, and beckon her inside. She moved in quickly, recognizing at once that they were within the music room, where some of the ladies had remained for most of the afternoon. "It is in here?" she asked, looking all about her as Lord Bentham hastily lit a few candles, so that they could see the room better. "Where?" She could see no hint of gold flickering in the room, no vase standing atop any surface. "Is it very small?"

Lord Bentham chuckled, then gestured toward the wall. "Do you see it now, Miss Seymour?"

With a gasp lodged in her throat, Hannah stepped closer, seeing the painting that Lord Bentham now pointed to. It was of a golden vase, which held some long-stemmed white flowers, drooping over the sides. It was quite lovely, but had he not pointed it out, she would have easily passed it by.

"How can there be another note in there?" she asked, frowning, coming to stand alongside Lord Bentham. "Do you think it is hidden behind it?"

Lord Bentham shrugged. "There is only one way to discover such a thing," he said, handing her a candle and then turning to pull a chair over toward the wall, so that he might reach the painting with a little more ease. "If you would be willing to assist, Miss Seymour?"

She did not hesitate but stepped forward at once, watching as he climbed onto the chair and then, with both hands, lifted the painting from the wall. It was not an overly large painting but she could tell that he was taking great care in moving it as slowly and as carefully as he could. Setting her candle down on a nearby table, Hannah reached up and took it from him, thinking to turn it over and look for a note, only to hear Lord Bentham's swift intake of breath.

She looked up and had to step back in astonishment, seeing that the picture had hidden what appeared to be a small safe.

"I did not know this was here," Lord Bentham breathed, half to himself. "Good gracious, my father..." He trailed off and said nothing more, shaking his head before he put his hand onto it. Hannah set the picture down carefully, then picked up her candle again, holding it aloft so that Lord Bentham might have a little more light to see. He cast her a grateful look, his eyes catching the glow of the flame for just a moment, before he pulled the small door open and looked inside.

Hannah pressed her lips together tightly, refusing to allow herself to ask any of the questions that now flooded her. This was Lord Bentham's house, Lord Bentham's safe, and Lord Bentham's responsibility. She would know soon enough what he had found.

"Papers."

His voice sounded dulled and he glanced down at her, his brow furrowed. "There are papers within, Miss Seymour."

She swallowed hard, wondering if this was the betrothal contract he had been searching for.

"And... wait." His voice held a tinge of excitement now as he reached inside the safe again, turning to look at her as he pulled out what appeared to be another white figurine. An exclamation left her lips as he held it out to her, bending carefully so that she might take it from him.

"Goodness!" she exclaimed, taking a hold of the figurine deftly and looking at it in the candlelight. "It is... not what I expected." The figurine was of a lady, yes, but she was much more portly than Hannah had thought she would be. In comparison to the gentleman figurine, she held none of the delicacy or refinement. There were no gentle lines but rather a hard sharpness that sent a shiver of dislike down Hannah's spine. In addition, the lady appeared to be a good deal bigger than the gentleman, which meant that they would have both been quite out of proportion with each other.

"Nor I," Lord Bentham agreed, climbing down from the chair, grasping the painting, and then standing back on the chair again so as to set it into place. "These papers, however..." Coming to stand by her, he set the papers down on the nearby table, unrolling them carefully. Hannah's stomach twisted as she looked down at the marriage contract, seeing the signature and the seal in both places.

It seemed there had been an agreement after all.

Lord Bentham let out a long breath, closing his eyes tightly. His hands flattened on the papers, his shoulders rounding and his head bending low, as if he were in great pain, one that he could not quite fully express.

"Lord Bentham," Hannah said, her throat dry, "I am... sorry that this is not what you hoped for."

Lord Bentham glanced up at her. "It does not make any difference," he told her as she struggled to find the will to believe him. "Miss Lewisham does not wish to marry me and I do not wish to marry her." Looking into her eyes, he put one hand over hers and then straightened. "I want to marry you."

Hannah swayed slightly at his words, overcome by the swell of emotion that crashed over her and the intensity of his gaze.

"Miss Seymour, I have been nothing but a fool," Lord Bentham continued, dropping his head for a moment. "I have broken your heart once before with my own selfishness and foolish ways only to realize what a scoundrel I have been." His head lifted and he looked into her eyes once more. Hannah set her candle down carefully, keeping her eyes on the flame for as long as she could so that she might regain a little composure.

"I held a regard for you that I chose to turn my back

on, not realizing just how precious a thing it was," Lord Bentham said, reaching out to take her hand, his fingers searing her skin with his gentle touch. "I come to you now in the hope that you might find a way to forgive me for what I have done, and to beg you to give me another chance." His other hand found her free one and held it tightly, his nearness making her catch her breath. "I would ask for your hand, Miss Seymour, with the promise that my heart will never again turn from you, seeking to remove itself from the affection that burns within it." His eyes melded to hers and Hannah found herself moving closer to him, so that they were only a few inches apart. Her heart ached with a desperate longing that burned her, that screamed at her to accept him, her breath hitching as his hand loosened from hers only to press to her cheek with infinite gentleness. "You are courageous, Miss Seymour, despite your fears that you have no strength within you. I have seen your deter-mination and your strength grow. I have seen you encourage Miss Lewisham, for you alone can truly understand the fear that comes with being ruled by a despot and a tyrant. And within that, I have seen how your own courage has blossomed, determined not to give in to your father's demands."

Hannah lifted her chin, feeling a new sense of pride envelop her. She *had* done as Lord Bentham now stated. She *had* determined that she would not go back to London, would not marry whoever her father had chosen for her, and in that newfound strength and courage, she had been able to find a way to encourage Miss Lewisham also.

"I admire you," Lord Bentham finished quietly. "I have an overwhelming desire to be near to you, to have you in my company almost every moment." Swallowing, he hesitated for a moment. "And I love you, Miss Seymour."

The room began to spin as she stared up at him, hardly believing that she had heard those words from his lips. She waited for him to take them back, to say that he had not meant to declare such a thing, only for him to smile with evident relief that he had managed to say the truth of what was in his heart, and to lift her hand to his mouth for a gentle kiss.

She was in his arms in a moment, her hands flung behind his neck and her mouth pressing to his, in place of where her hand had just been. Lord Bentham staggered backwards for a moment, only to pull her tightly against him and to angle his head, his lips burning like fire as he pressed them to hers. Her heart soared as he kissed her, tears of happiness creeping into her eyes as she kissed him with all that she felt, allowing the pain of the past to fall away completely, forgiveness and hope filling the wounds that had been struck so many weeks before.

"Miss Seymour." Lord Bentham pulled back, his forehead resting on hers, his breathing quick. "Miss

Seymour, might I hope that this means...?" He did not finish his sentence, looking earnestly into her eyes, and Hannah reached back so that she might cup his face in her hands.

"It would be a fulfilment of my greatest wish, Lord Bentham," she told him quietly, a beautiful smile crossing her lips. "Yes, Lord Bentham. Yes, I will marry you. I will be your wife."

"And I shall never cease in my love for you," he told her, before bending his head to kiss her again.

The sudden sound of a door crashing back into the wall had them jerking apart in an instant, as a roar of anger burned in Hannah's ears. Flushing and embarrassed, she turned her head away, just as Miss Lewisham, Lord Greene, and the rest of The Shadows poured into the music room, with Miss Hawkins hurrying to her side and catching her arm.

"Lord Bentham!" Lord Greene shouted, his anger clearly visible. "Did you really think you could leave your guests without someone noticing that you had gone?" His eyes traveled toward Hannah, his lip curling. "Taking your pleasures where you will, I see."

Hannah flushed with mortification and turned away, only for Lord Bentham to step toward her. Looking down into her face, he took her hand and then lifted his eyes back toward Lord Greene.

"I am in love with Miss Seymour," he said firmly, as a

few gasps came from the others present. "I intend to marry her."

Hannah watched Lord Greene intently, feeling a little more emboldened now that she had both Lord Bentham and Miss Hawkins by her side. Lord Greene's expression was dark, his eyes flicking from one side of the room to the other, before landing on the papers on the table in front of Hannah. She moved quickly, snatching them up—but not before Lord Greene had seen precisely what was upon them.

"The papers!" he cried as Hannah handed them quickly to Lord Bentham. "You have them." He chuckled malevolently, with a strangled sob coming from Miss Lewisham's throat. "Then it is settled. The marriage will take place."

Hannah's throat closed up as she looked at Lord Bentham, then back to Miss Lewisham. Closing her eyes, she let out a long breath and then opened them again, looking fixedly at Lord Greene.

"There will be no marriage," she said firmly. "Lord Bentham had, just now, proposed to me and I have accepted. In addition," she continued, her voice rising as Lord Greene began to splutter, "your niece does not wish to marry Lord Bentham either. We know precisely why you have been pushing for this marriage, Lord Greene." Stepping forward, she picked up the figurine, which had lain unnoticed by Lord Greene until this very moment. "You do not care about your niece, sir," she said loudly. "You have only sought to find this. Miss Lewisham has been instructed to find it and return it to you. Is that not so?"

Lord Greene scowled but took a heavy step forward, one hand held out. "That belongs to me," he said with such a sense of determination that had she been a weaker sort, Hannah might have given him the figurine without question. "It was a promise made by my brother and should be returned to us now."

"I hardly think so," Hannah said stiffly, holding the figurine close to her chest. "What is it about this lady that you care about so much, Lord Greene?" She tipped her head, noticing how one or two of The Shadows now sat down behind Lord Greene, easily able to block his path should he attempt to escape the room. "Why do you want her?"

Lord Greene narrowed his eyes. "It is to be returned to my family when the marriage takes place," he said, without giving her any answers to any of her questions. "Do so now, Miss Seymour."

Lord Bentham's audible gasp caught everyone's attention. When she looked to him, she saw Lord Bentham staring down at one of the papers as though he had never seen it before. She was all the more astonished when he sat down heavily in a chair, his eyes still fixed to the words as though they were stuck there without any ability to remove themselves from it.

"Lord Bentham?" she asked, only for the door to

open and, much to their astonishment, Lord Paxton to step inside. He was soon followed by a dark-haired lady, whose eyes were huge with fright. Miss Lewisham let out a scream of relief and ran toward her, embracing her mother with such strength that Hannah feared the poor lady would be quite robbed of breath. Lord Haddington came in after Lady Greene and shut the door with a firm click, one eyebrow lifted as he looked at the scene before him.

"What the devil are you doing here?"

Lord Greene was on his feet, his eyes wide and staring as he looked at his sister-in-law, clearly overcome with shock to see her there. "How did you—?"

"Would you believe it?" Lord Paxton interrupted mildly, looking at Hannah and Lord Bentham rather than at Lord Greene. "We discovered a lady of quality riding alone toward the estate." He gestured to Lady Greene. "It appears she knew that her daughter was present here, thanks to a letter that had been delivered from Miss Lewisham, and so decided to find a way to escape the Dower house and make her way here."

Hannah stared at the older lady but found her heart swelling with admiration and relief. "Goodness," she murmured as Miss Lewisham wept great tears of gladness into her mother's shoulder. "It seems she has more determination within her than perhaps even Miss Lewisham thought."

"It appears so," Lord Paxton replied with a satisfied

smile, sitting down in a chair and settling back into it. "We have told her everything, Lord Bentham, so she is fully aware of all that is going on at present, although I did promise her rest and a good deal of food when she arrived in order to build up her strength a little more." His eyes darted back toward Lady Greene, who was now being shown to a chair by her daughter. "I think it took a good deal from her to escape as she did."

Hannah rang the bell immediately, watching Lord Greene, who appeared to balloon as he stood by his chair, his hands curled into tight, angry fists. Her stomach tightened with nervousness, aware of how both Lady Greene and Miss Lewisham were steadfastly avoiding Lord Greene's gaze. She came to stand next to Lord Bentham again, putting her hand on his arm.

"I will speak to the maid when she arrives," she told him in a low voice, aware of the gratitude radiating from his eyes. "Should we send for Lord Kerr?"

Lord Bentham shook his head. "Not yet," he said, his eyes drifting toward the papers he still held in his hands. "I have discovered something of the greatest importance. Once Lady Greene has been brought what she needs, I will speak to everyone about what my father has left me." There was a measure of sadness in his eyes and he reached up to cup her cheek for a moment. "Finally, I can understand the reason behind his decision to hide these clues from me. It seems there is more to this than perhaps even Lady Greene knows."

Hannah held his gaze, hearing the questions ringing in her mind but keeping them from her mouth as she nodded. Lord Bentham dropped his hand and cleared his throat, just as a scratch came at the door.

"Sit down, Lord Greene," Lord Bentham said purposefully as Hannah hurried to the door, directing the maid to bring refreshments and anything left from this evening's dinner to serve their unexpected guest. "There is much to disclose and I think everyone present needs to hear what I have to say." Hannah saw his eyes move toward Lady Greene and then to Miss Lewisham. "Lady Greene, I commend you for your bravery. I understand that your brother-in-law has, thus far, refused to permit you to leave the Dower house, keeping you practically under guard."

Lady Greene nodded and, as she spoke, Hannah could see the weariness in her features. Her eyes were heavy, the lines in her forehead etched deeply as her brow furrowed. Her voice was quiet and she did not even glance toward Lord Greene—who was, Hannah noted, still on his feet.

"That is quite true, Lord Bentham," Lady Greene said hoarsely. "But when I received my daughter's letter, I forced myself to find a way to escape and to come to her here. Your estate is not so far from the house and I—"

"You have no right to be here," Lord Greene interrupted, his voice grating. "I instructed you—"

"You are a tyrant, Lord Greene!" Lady Haddington's voice rang out, interrupting Lord Greene and sending him spiraling backwards as he turned to face her. "It is *you* who is in the wrong here. A gentleman is expected to care for his family in consideration and love, whereas you have flung your sister-in-law into one house as though it is a prison and thereafter used your niece in order to secure something that is of evidently great importance to you—although we are yet to discover that significance." She arched one eyebrow as Hannah sank down into a chair, looking to Lord Bentham, who was still gripping the papers. "Do not think that you can rule over us here with your anger and fury. It will not be accepted and we will not bow to you."

"No, we shall not," Miss Lewisham squeaked as Hannah caught her eye, giving her a quick smile of encouragement. "I have had enough, Uncle. I will not do as you demand any longer. And even if this agreement stands, I shall not marry Lord Bentham. Not when I know he loves another and when I myself have no wish to do so."

Lord Greene growled low in his throat, his face beginning to redden. "You will do as I say," he gritted out, beginning to advance toward his niece. "Else you will find yourself—"

"Sit down, Lord Greene," Lord Bentham stepped forward, directly into Lord Greene's path. "Sit down and be silent." He pointed one finger directly into Lord

Greene's chest, his eyes narrowing. "I have found you out," he continued, his voice a little quieter now but filled with meaning. "And I intend to tell everyone here the truth. You have no power any longer, Lord Greene. The time for you to speak has come to an end."

11

———————

George's heart was thumping furiously but he kept his gaze firm and his finger pressed against Lord Greene's chest. His narrowed eyes and his hard words eventually seemed to have the desired effect, for Lord Greene let out a heavy breath, muttered darkly under his breath, and then stepped back, slumping into a chair and averting his eyes. George, seeing the maid now frozen at the back of the room, standing by the door, lifted his chin and beckoned her in, waiting until trays had been set before Miss Lewisham and Lady Greene, with three other trays set out by the other maids for the rest of those present. Lord Paxton got up lazily and wandered to the drinks tray, pouring a brandy for himself and then gesturing toward the other gentlemen to see if they would like one also.

George shook his head. He wanted to have complete

control of his senses. Aware of the growing tension in the room, he took a breath and sat back down in his chair, the papers still in his lap.

"When I first met Lord Greene," he began, keeping his voice low and steady, "he came to tell me that I was engaged to his niece, Miss Lewisham." He gave the lady a smile and saw her nod, her face pale and yet a growing determination in her eyes. "I had never heard of such a betrothal and yet the papers presented to me appeared to be quite real."

"Although they lacked your father's seal," Miss Seymour interrupted, as though he might have forgotten. "That was why you did not accept the betrothal immediately."

Lord Greene snorted and muttered something under his breath, although he did not quite meet George's gaze. Apparently, he now knew that George understood precisely all that was to come.

"That is quite correct, Miss Seymour," George said calmly. "I thought to come to search for them here, only to discover that I was to host a house party." Lord Haddington chuckled, sharing a glance with Lord Paxton. "I will not pretend that I was a little overwhelmed, but I am grateful for it now. To have The Shadows here to help me with my search, to assist me in sorting out the confusion that surrounded us all..." He smiled at each of them, ignoring Lord Greene's puzzled look. "I am grateful to all of you for what you have done.

In discovering the clues my father left me—quite by chance, I will confess—I have realized now that I was meant to know of this betrothal a long time ago. I was meant to have sought you out, Miss Lewisham. I was meant to have done my duty by you in order to protect you and bring you into the family that you were always meant to have had."

Lady Greene let out a startled gasp, her hand flying to her mouth as she stared at him. George smiled gently, only for Lady Greene's eyes to fill with tears, a single one trickling down her cheek. Miss Lewisham, horrified, wrapped one arm about her mother's shoulder and murmured something soothing, but Lady Greene only covered her face with her hands and let out a heart-breaking sob.

"You need not be upset, Lady Greene," George said reassuringly. "I will not speak of what I have discovered, if you do not wish me to do so."

Lady Greene accepted the handkerchief her daughter held out to her, wiping her eyes before lifting her eyes to his. There was such sadness there that George felt his own heart sting with pain, holding her gaze steadily and waiting until she had made her decision.

"No, Lord Bentham," Lady Greene said eventually, her voice barely loud enough for him to hear. "I have seen my daughter suffer enough already. Please." She gestured with one hand, waving it toward him. "Continue."

Knowing that every eye was on him, George cleared his throat and picked up the first of the papers. "This is the betrothal agreement," he said as it slowly unrolled. "It has both signatures and both seals."

"Then the agreement has been made," Lord Greene declared angrily. "There is no need for any further discussion."

George ignored this completely and continued. "I believe that my father deliberately did not put his seal on the papers that were held by Lord Greene, however. I think this was for the specific reason that I would search for *his* papers and, in doing so, I would discover the truth."

"And what is that?" Lady Ann asked, leaning forward in her seat, her teacup already forgotten. "What have you discovered?"

Hesitating, George looked at Lady Greene and saw her nod almost imperceptibly. This was going to hurt Miss Lewisham greatly, he knew, but it had to be said, regardless.

"It appears, Miss Lewisham," he began, setting down the betrothal papers on the table and pulling out another one, "that you are not Lord Greene's daughter."

Silence filled the room and George swallowed hard, feeling the tension mounting furiously as everyone stared back at him. Miss Lewisham went sheet-white, her fingers grasping her mother's arm, her eyes wide and staring.

"I should, perhaps, have told you the truth some time ago," Lady Greene whispered tremulously, "but I could never bring myself to do so." A sob escaped her, but she controlled herself with an effort, for the sake of her daughter. "Sarah, your father was not Lord Greene. He married me when you were but a few months old and from that day, took on the duty of a parent." Her eyes swam with tears and George dared a look toward Miss Lewisham's uncle, seeing the dark fury on his face and knowing full well that the man knew everything that was going on. "He was, in every other sense, your father, but he was not your kin."

Miss Lewisham said nothing for some minutes, clearly too shocked to speak. Miss Seymour stared at him, clearly completely astonished at this news, whilst the other Shadows looked with a mixture of sympathy and surprise toward Miss Lewisham.

"I do not understand," Miss Lewisham whispered, one hand pressed to her heart and the other hand holding tightly to her mother. "Who was my father?" She swallowed hard. "Does he still live?"

Lady Greene shook her head and Miss Lewisham dropped her head.

"Your father, my dear girl, was a loving man who cared very deeply for me," Lady Greene said, her expression one of deep sadness as her eyes grew wistful, thinking about what had gone on in the past. "I loved him and he loved me, but our union was not one that my own father approved of. My husband was not rich nor was he titled, but I was contented in our quiet living." A tear tracked down her cheek but still, a smile crossed her face as she looked at her daughter. "When he knew that I was with child, he was so delighted that he could barely speak. He took great care of you when you were born, filled with such a love for you that I knew he would care for you for the rest of your days."

"And then, he passed away," George said softly, seeing the wretchedness on Lady Greene's face. "Unexpectedly so?"

"Very unexpectedly," Lady Greene said, nodding. "It was a tragic accident. A gentleman riding along the road went much too fast and knocked him to the ground." She began to cry in earnest, evidently recalling what had occurred. "I was present, carrying you in my arms, Sarah. When the gentleman realized what he had done, he took a pouch from his pocket and threw it toward me, in evident recompense for what he had done. Then he rode away and I did not ever see him again."

Lady Haddington sucked in a breath, her eyes wide. "You mean to say, you did not know his name? He did not return to help? To aid you with the dreadful thing that had occurred?"

Lady Greene shook her head, closing her eyes tightly, her skin taut over her hollow cheeks, appearing almost waxen as she recalled her grief. "Indeed, he did not," she said hoarsely. "And thus, I was left alone with a child on the road, my husband dead before me and no understanding of what I was to do next."

George nodded, seeing how Miss Lewisham pressed her mother's hand, her color a little improved. "And so, you turned to your father."

"I had no other choice," Lady Greene said, her voice finally growing a little stronger. "I fell on his mercy and he did not turn away from me as I had feared."

"What did he do?" Miss Lewisham asked, looking directly into her mother's face and waiting to hear what Lady Greene had to say. "How did he help you?"

Lady Greene's smile was gentle. "He found a husband for me," she said softly. "A husband who, I am afraid, required money in return for marrying me and taking on my child as his own. Money my father was willing to give. He cleared his debts and thus, in turn, the marriage was arranged."

"And this gentleman was Lord Greene," Miss Seymour murmured, and Lady Greene nodded. "And he treated you well?"

Lady Greene's smile grew. "He did," she answered fervently. "I will confess that at first, there was a good deal of anxiety and tension between us, but it was you, Sarah, who captured his heart first." She squeezed her daughter's hand, turning to her a little more. "He loved you as though you were his own. And, in turn, that love for you grew to encompass me also. I was very blessed indeed to become his wife."

George watched Miss Lewisham closely, seeing her chest rise and fall as she took in a deep breath. Her eyes closed and for a moment, he worried that she might faint, only to see her open her eyes and looked fixedly back at him, her newfound strength now evident.

"Then how is your father involved?" she asked, her gaze clear. "How did he come to know of all of this?"

George looked down at the letter and let out a long breath, looking up at Miss Lewisham and feeling his heart begin to pound furiously. "Miss Lewisham, the man your mother married first—your father—was brother to my own father."

This pronouncement brought yet another gasp of shock from the group, with Miss Seymour starting violently as he spoke. Miss Lewisham said nothing, nor did her stance change. She simply nodded slowly, looking at her mother, who gave her a weak smile.

"This means that we are cousins, Miss Lewisham," George continued after a few moments. "My father has written that the arrangement of marriage was made so that your future would be secure. However, he has also stated that if such a marriage is less than desirous, he gives me the responsibility to find you a suitable match in his place." A small shrug lifted his shoulders. "After all, not everyone within society is glad to see cousins marrying." He shot a glance toward Lord Greene. "It is also noted in this letter that Lord Greene—your adoptive father, Miss Lewisham—was suspicious of his brother. The brother who would inherit the title and the estate, should he pass away."

Lord Greene let out a harsh laugh, his features twisted. "Why should he have any reason to doubt me?"

"Because," George said, looking down at the letter and seeing what his father had written there, "he knew that you wanted what had been given to Lady Greene when she had first lost her husband." He lifted his gaze and pinned it tightly to Lord Greene, whose brows lowered, his eyes flint. "Lady Greene did not want them, did not want to keep what had been flung at her by the gentleman who had taken her husband from her. And thus, when Lord Greene took her as his wife and stepped into the role of Miss Lewisham's father, he was tasked with what he ought to do."

"I did not know what he did with them, nor did I want to know," Lady Greene added, her eyes also holding a flicker of anger. "Not after what had happened."

Miss Lewisham looked from one to the other her eyes holding a myriad of questions. "What was it that you were given, Mama?" she asked, a note of desperation in her voice. "What did Lord Greene hide?"

"He told you once, did he not?" George asked mildly, turning to Lord Greene. "And soon came to regret his decision, given your reaction."

Lord Greene glowered at him, his lips pulled tight and no response coming from his mouth.

"You wanted them for yourself. You tried to find any way you could to get them for yourself." George shook his head. "Lord Greene did not tell you what he had done with them, but you must have discovered the truth."

Lord Greene's lip curled. "His papers provided the answer."

George nodded slowly. "So, once your brother passed away, you began to search through his papers and discovered the truth. Did you know that he had gone to such lengths so that he could hide them from you?" He glanced down at the paper, reading the words aloud. "It says here that 'Lord Greene has taken great lengths to hide such a treasure for fear that his brother will seek them out one way or the other. Only he and I, at present, know what he has done with them.'" His gaze narrowed with dislike. "When you found out the truth, you discovered that he had hidden them in figurines. You knew that the key was in the one that Miss Lewisham had, but not where the other was. How glad you must have been when the papers were found, indicating that Miss Lewisham was to marry me. You knew then that your brother had placed the other figurine in this house."

"And that is why your own father took such great pains to hide this all from the rest of the world," Miss

Seymour said quietly, her eyes filled with wonderment. "It was to be kept a secret from the world—even from yourself—unless there came reason for you to wed."

George nodded. "Such a thing also had to be mentioned in his will, in case he died before he had either need or opportunity to tell me about the arrangement." He shrugged. "After all, if Miss Lewisham had married before her father had passed away, then the arrangement would have been voided."

"But then the diamonds would have remained with you."

Another gasp rippled around the room as Lord Greene threw himself out of the chair, one hand pointed toward George, fingers trembling. His shoulders were raised, his eyes dark and narrowed.

"Diamonds?" Miss Lewisham whispered, again grasping her mother's hand tightly. "You were given diamonds, Mama?"

Lady Greene nodded, her lips white. "I did not want them," she rasped, her words bitter. "To be given such precious things in the place of one life..." She shook her head, her eyes closed tightly. "I did not want a single one. Nothing could have brought me any relief or contentment over your father's death, Sarah."

George nodded in understanding. "And so, Lord Greene gave them to my father, knowing that we were related," he explained. "But he gave them in the hope that they would one day be returned to you, so that you, Miss Lewisham, would have the choice of what to do."

Miss Seymour reached forward, picked up the figurine, and with one swift motion, flung it down onto the hearth just behind George. Lord Greene let out a scream of disapproval, but George rose at once and held him back, seeing Miss Seymour picking up a small wooden box.

"Goodness," Miss Seymour murmured as she walked to Miss Lewisham, handing it to her. "Your adoptive father went to great lengths to keep such a thing hidden, Miss Lewisham." She cast an angry glance toward Lord Greene. "And I can well understand why."

Miss Lewisham blinked in surprise, looking over the box carefully. "The key in one and the diamonds in the other," she whispered as Miss Seymour handed her the small key that she had kept in her pocket. "My dear papa was a prudent gentleman." Her eyes darted toward her uncle. "He knew the characters of those around him and sought to protect me from them."

Pushing the key into the lock, Miss Lewisham turned it carefully. It took a moment, sticking for a second or two, before turning completely. Turning the box in her hand so that the key stood pointing to the ceiling, Miss Lewisham pulled the small lid back and caught her breath.

"Diamonds," she whispered, unable to take her gaze

from them. "Just as you said, Lord Bentham. The diamonds are here."

George walked over toward her and looked down at the small box in her hand, awed at the sight of the diamonds held there, sparkling and catching the light with a vibrance that took his breath away. Miss Lewisham looked up at him, questioningly, and he smiled at her with both kindness and understanding.

"They are yours to do with as you please, Miss Lewisham," he said quietly. "The agreement was to be that they would be returned to you once we were wed— and, if we were not, then I was to make you aware of their existence at an appropriate time." He shrugged, feeling the heavy burden of responsibility on his shoulders. "Not that I am certain I could have done such a thing with any great ease."

"You have done very well, Lord Bentham," Lady Greene whispered, clearly overcome with all that she felt at present. "I thank you."

He inclined his head. "I would not tell you what you ought to do with these diamonds, Miss Lewisham," he said, turning back to his cousin. "But as we are now family, I will give you a little advice."

Miss Lewisham nodded, her smile a little watery as she looked up expectantly. George bent down, looking into his cousin's face and wondering if she would have enough strength to do as he was about to suggest.

"You are not under your uncle's rule any longer, Miss

Lewisham," he said softly. "You are not his blood. I understand that your first desire might be to rid yourself of these precious jewels, but there is an opportunity here to use them for your good—and for that of your mother also." He glanced toward Lady Greene, whose lips were trembling but who, after a moment, gave a small nod. "Lord Kerr has offered you his hand in marriage, I understand," he continued. "That may be a wise decision—I cannot say—but what you have in your hand can be used to ensure that you have the time to make such a decision wisely, Miss Lewisham. Take care of your mother."

"If you go with that daughter of yours—a girl who is not even *kin* to me—then you shall *never* be allowed back under my roof!" Lord Greene roared, the room seeming to shake from the fury of his words. "Do you hear me? You shall never again be permitted to—"

"That is quite enough, Lord Greene."

With a strength that George did not think Miss Lewisham possessed, the lady rose and strode toward her guardian, her head held high.

"You have used me ill," she said, her voice shaking but loud enough for them all to hear. "My mother does not need your house, your estate, or your wealth. *I* shall be by her side and she shall be by mine. These diamonds are not yours, Lord Greene, nor shall they ever be." She lifted her chin and looked into his eyes, her back ramrod straight. Silently, George rose to his feet, seeing the others do the same. The Shadows came together as one, standing by Miss Lewisham as though they were protecting her, standing together so that she would not have to stand alone. George could see the determination shining in Miss Seymour's eyes and knew that the strength that had been building within her would never be lost now.

"And I do not think you are welcome in this house any longer," Miss Seymour said, throwing a glance toward George, who nodded empathically. "Leave, Lord Greene. And do not even attempt to command Lady Greene or Miss Lewisham to accompany you, for they shall not."

"I shall not." Lady Greene rose, her frame shaking, yet with a courage that defied her weakness. She glared at her brother-in-law, her head held high. "I will no longer be held captive in the Dower house, afraid to do as you ask. I found a way to escape from the guards you had set there, forced myself to find the strength I needed to return to my daughter, fearful of what you had done to her. I shall never go back to your house now. Never!"

George watched in satisfaction as Lord Greene began to stammer, his bluster and his arrogance gone in a moment. He stepped back, just as Lord Haddington opened the door and stood by it, gesturing for him to walk through. George smiled to himself and walked toward Miss Seymour, aware that every gaze was fixed on Lord Greene. Silence reigned until, finally, Lord

Greene staggered out of the room, no longer the bold, angry gentleman who had first stepped through.

A great sigh erupted from every lip as the door was closed firmly on Lord Greene. Miss Lewisham turned at once toward her mother, holding her tightly as tears began to run down almost every cheek.

"You are, of course, welcome to remain here for as long as you wish," George said warmly, as Lady Greene wept all the more. "And Miss Lewisham, you are welcome also. Although," he added with a slightly wry grin, "you may have a little explaining to do when it comes to Lord Kerr."

Miss Lewisham laughed through her tears, and George felt a hand touch his arm. Looking down, he saw Miss Seymour standing beside him, her face aglow with love, and felt his heart soar toward the skies. He was more contented than he had ever been before, free of his burdens, stepping away from confusion. He hoped that all that was left for them now was happiness.

Hannah wrapped her arms around herself in satisfaction as she watched Lord Greene's carriage roll away from the Bentham estate. She let out a long breath, smiling to herself as she watched it round the bend, glad beyond all explanation that her friend, Miss Lewisham, was now safe from her uncle's demands. Lady Greene also was now sitting contentedly with her daughter, her expression relaxed and her face wreathed in smiles. Miss Lewisham, now a little relieved of her shock and surprise with all that had taken place, was smiling and laughing with the other Shadows, which was an expression that Hannah had not seen on Miss Lewisham's face before. There was a freedom there now, a freedom that Hannah hoped would continue for the rest of Miss Lewisham's life. Lord Kerr was present also, talking to the Shadows and to Miss Lewisham. Whilst shocked, he was standing by Miss Lewisham and Hannah had every reason to hope that in time, his marriage to Miss Lewisham would take place.

"Hannah?"

It was the gentle, tender voice she had come to know so well. The way he spoke her name, with an almost reverent touch to his voice, made her heart swell with happiness, her hands clasping together as she turned to face him.

"Lord Bentham," she murmured, her eyes fixing to his in an instant, seeing the flickering light in those blue orbs as he smiled at her. "It is over, then."

"It is," he said, reaching for her hand and pressing it gently. "And now I can think of the future and all that it might contain."

Hannah caught her breath with the promise in his eyes, moving toward him—only for Lord Bentham to step to one side and then tug her along beside him, a grin on his handsome face as he led her from the room. She leaned into him, feeling his arm settling on her waist as they walked together, not knowing where they were going but trusting him entirely.

"Do you think I should speak to your father?"

Lord Bentham slowed his steps and pulled her gently into the parlor, which, Hannah saw, was entirely empty. Her heart turned over in her chest as he reached out and cupped her cheek, the tender gesture softening her all the more.

"My father does not care much for me, Lord Bentham," she said honestly. "I do not know if I have ever spoken to you of what he has demanded of me, but I shall tell you now, if you would wish to hear it?"

Lord Bentham's hand dropped to her shoulder but he nodded, his eyes suddenly serious. "I have been told that you have had some struggles," he said quietly, "but I have not known the specific difficulties of it."

Hannah swallowed, her happiness a little dampened. Quickly, she told him of her father's demands, telling him of just how certain she was that her father intended to wed her to someone that would be entirely for his own benefit. "Lady Haddington has asked me to reside with her for a time, when this house party ends," she finished, feeling that newfound sense of strength growing up within her again. "Initially, I was too afraid to agree, but now that I have seen what Miss Lewisham has faced and overcome, I have found a courage within my heart that I do not think will ever leave me." She smiled at him and saw the pride in his expression as he looked back at her, his lips pulled up on one side, his eyes glowing. "Therefore, if it is required of me, I shall return with Lady Haddington."

"It shall *not* be required," he said, stepping closer so that his head was only a few inches away from her own, his arms pulling her tightly against him. "You have said you will marry me, Hannah. Is that still the desire of your heart?"

Tipping her head back, she looked deeply into his eyes. "It is," she told him ardently. "The past is forgotten. I have seen your regret and your sorrow and I trust your heart, Lord Bentham. You say you love me and I feel that very same love in return." Reaching up, she ran her fingers down over his cheek, just as he had done to her. "My only wish is to be your wife, Lord Bentham. Not because I wish to escape from my father's plans but because my heart is yours."

Bending his head, he brushed a kiss over her lips, sparks flying all through her as he did so. "Then say you will run away with me, Hannah," he whispered, laughing softly at the astonishment in her face. "The border to Scotland is not all that far away. We can be married there and you need never return to your father again."

She laughed in delight, throwing her hands around his neck and feeling her heart fill with overwhelming joy. "Yes," she cried, her hands brushing through his hair at the nape of his neck. "Yes, George, I will run away with you."

His lips were warm, his kiss one of hope and passion. "Then shall we go, my love?" he whispered against her lips. "I would make you my wife this very day."

She kissed him back, her answer apparent in that

kiss. He held her close for a moment longer, then stepped back and held out his hand to her. Hannah took it at once and together, they quit the room, their pace hurried and their hearts filled with eagerness as they took their first steps together to becoming husband and wife.

~

What to Read Next?

<u>Brides of London: Regency Romance Collection</u>
Four romances to make you fall in love with the lords and ladies of Regency England. Discover love, mystery, suspense, and scandals in this heartwarming collection.

LOVE LIGHT FAITH

Receive a FREE inspirational romance eBook by visiting our website and signing up for our mailing list. Click the link or enter www.LoveLightFaith.com into your browser.

The newsletter will also provide information on upcoming books and special offers.

MORE STORIES YOU'LL LOVE

If you loved reading this book, discover other clean romances that will warm your heart.

<u>Brides of London: Regency Romance Collection</u>
Four Regency romances filled with mystery, suspense, and surprising twists.

<u>Weddings and Scandals: Regency Romance Collection</u>
Four Regency romances filled with mystery, suspense, and surprising twists.

<u>Seasons of Brides: Regency Romance Collection</u>
Would you give up everything for the one you love?

<u>Hearts and Ever Afters: Regency Romance Collection</u>

Heartwarming Regency romances filled with mystery, intrigue, surprising twists, and of course, love!

Secrets of London: Regency Romance Collection
Secrets. Love. Mystery. Romance. Join the lords and ladies of Regency England in this heartwarming romance collection.

Gentlemen and Brides: Regency Romance Collection
Fall in love with the lords and ladies of Regency England in this inspirational romance collection.

THANK YOU!

Thank you for reading this book! Avid readers like you make an author's world shine.

If you've enjoyed this book, or any other books by Joyce Alec, please don't hesitate to review them on Amazon or Goodreads. Every single review makes an incredible difference. The reason for this is simple: other readers trust reviews more than professional endorsements. For this reason, we rely on our readers to spread the good word.

Sending you endless appreciation, plus a little love, light and faith!